AF730239

THE BOOK OF
A HUNDRED HANDS

THE BOOK OF
A HUNDRED HANDS

By
GEORGE B. BRIDGMAN

INSTRUCTOR IN DRAWING AND
LECTURER ON THE CONSTRUCTION
AND ANATOMY OF THE HUMAN
FIGURE, ART STUDENTS' LEAGUE
NEW YORK
AUTHOR OF CONSTRUCTIVE
ANATOMY

KALPAZ

©Reserved

All rights reserved. No part of this work may be reproduced, stored, adapted, or transmitted in any form or by any means, electronic, mechanical, photocopying, micro-filming recording or otherwise, or translated in any language, without the prior written permission of the copyright owner and the publisher. The book is sold subject to the condition that it shall not, by way of trade or otherwise, be lent, resold, hired out, or otherwise circulated without the prior publisher's written consent in any form of binding or cover other than that in which it is published.

The views and opinions expressed in this book are author(s) own and the facts reported by them have been verified to the extent possible, and the publishers are not in any way liable for the same.

ISBN: 978-93-5128-417-8(HB)

First Published in 1920
Indian Reprint in 2017

Published by

Kalpaz Publications
C-30, Satyawati Nagar,
Delhi – 110052
E-mail: kalpaz@hotmail.com
Website: kalpazpublications.com
Ph.: +91-9212142040

Dedicated
to
Helene

THE AUTHOR desires to acknowledge his indebtedness to Dr. Ernest E. Tucker as his collaborator in the preparation of this volume.

G. B. B.

Introduction

Helvétius, in 1758, in an essay on "The Mind," quoted by H. T. Buckle in his "Introduction to the History of Civilization," maintains as an incontrovertible fact that the difference between man and animal is a result of the difference in their external form; that if for example the wrists instead of ending in hands with flexible fingers had ended like a horse's hoof, man would have remained a wanderer on the face of the earth among the animals, ignorant of every art and entirely defenseless; that this structure—the hand—is the sole cause of our superiority.

Ever since the genesis of the human race, the hand has been the indispensible instrument of its continued advance. About the creations of this hand, in science and in art, an endless succession of volumes has been written; to the hand, also, many scientific works are devoted; but the writer has not discovered a single volume devoted exclusively to the depicting of the hand.

It is the purpose of this work to present the hand not only to the eye, but to the understanding.

History of the Hand in Art

Nature standardizes all hands to laws of mechanics and dynamics. The hands of the mummies of ancient Egypt, thousands of years old, are not different from those of today. The bones of prehistoric man are the same. Ninety per cent., and more, of the hand is standardized by its use to the unchanging laws of its use.

But the hand as drawn and sculptured has varied markedly in different ages. Cave dwellers marked the walls and roofs of their dwellings and their implements with signs and figures, and among them, hands. The hands they drew or carved had a general character distinctly of that age.

The Peruvian, the Aztec, the American Indian in his written sign language, the Alaskan on his totem pole, each of these—whether the hand was carved out or cut in, drawn or painted, in red or blue, wherever a hand was shown—adhered to a certain style of hand whose character marked it as belonging to that age or that tribe or that race, and all distinctly different from other periods or races or tribes.

The Assyrians graved hands on their palace walls and carved them in stone; and they were Assyrian hands, distinguishable easily from those of any other race or age. The Egyptians told stories by means of carved and painted hands, as individual as those of any other place or time.

When we come to the ages of a more studied art, the same psychological law is in evidence. There is an early Gothic hand, distinctly different from that of any other period.

There is a Renaissance hand with a character of its own; so much so that they can be picked out and classified, not only as Renaissance hands, but as early or late Renaissance hands.

No one questions the sincerity of Ghirlandajo, or of Lippi, or of Botticelli. Not only were they great masters, but close students, and yet each drew a different style of hand.

Of later schools the same thing may be said; as of the Venetian and the Dutch schools, and of the schools of Jordaens, Rubens and Van Dyck. Of Van Dyck it has been said that he could not draw the hand of a laborer, and of Millet that he could not draw a gentleman's hand.

Indeed, it is very far from accurate to say that we see with our eyes. The eye is blind but for the idea behind the eye. It is the idea behind the eye that makes it different from a photographic plate—that pricks out some parts with emphasis and censors other parts. We see with the idea, and only *through* the eye.

Michaël Angelo, Leonardo Da Vinci and Raphael, all of the same period, all had the same style of models, and yet they produced hands of three very distinct types.

Albert Dürer, Holbein the younger, Rembrandt, all made hands that, because of their individuality, are classed as a Holbein or a Dürer or a Rembrandt hand by the art world.

Reasons for this change and flux in character and style of hands are no doubt familiar to every one. Briefly, the hand as pictured is not subject to the automatic forces that standardize the actual hand to the laws of its use. The pictured hand is standardized to no laws except those of perception: which means to the current concepts and to individual taste. The business of the artist in such a connection is to standardize his concepts of the hand to those of nature—to see it as nature sees its purpose, methods, laws.

It may be reflected that the science of anatomy is a comparatively recent acquisition of the race. It is not many decades since the cutting up of the human body was forbidden by law and abhorred in religion. Even after such a study is well developed, it takes a certain time for its significance to penetrate to other domains of thought and effort, and a much longer time for it to be assimilated there.

It has taken man centuries to learn to look under the form for the mechanisms in the human body; and he is only now learning to look under the mechanisms for the reasons that underlie them. The world of art is beginning to appropriate these things to itself, and the improvement in one man's technic by this means compels others to seek improvement in the same school—the school of nature, her reasons and her purposes.

If this tendency to fluctuations, to styles and fashions is more marked in the hand than in other parts of the body, it is probably because the importance of the hand as an avenue of expression has not been understood. The hand is thought of as the slave of action. But the slave of action is the master of expression.

Expression

The face is well schooled to self-control as a rule, and may become an aid in dissimulation of thought and feeling.

Rarely is the hand so trained; and responding unconsciously to the mental states, it may reveal what the face would conceal.

Like any other living thing, the hand is modified to its use. The total modification in any individual is less than one per cent.; but in a succession of generations it may be cumulative. Also it happens that it is the more superficial and conspicuous parts that are thus modified.

On the background of the mechanics, then, which is older than the human race, we may have racial variations; then on this basis, accumulated hereditary or family modifications, and on them in turn expressions of individual history and character.

The hand of the child is almost unmodified. With its creases and dimples and its tapering fingers, it represents almost the pure symmetry that is the natural heritage of all created things.

The hand of age represents the opposite extreme, the end product, the insanity of over-modification; furrowed, wrinkled with the scars of time, with enlarged squared joints, and shaky.

On the background then of mechanics and racial variations, we have many variations, such as those of youth or age; male or female; healthy or unsound; laboring or aristocratic; strong or weak.

Types of hands may be classified as: square, round, compact; long or short; thick or thin. The relative length of fingers varies, both among themselves and in comparison with the hand. The relative thickness of joint and shaft and finger tip varies. The thumb may be short, thick or thin, may lie close or spread far from the hand.

The hand that is inured to heavy labor shows very definite changes. It is larger and heavier. The muscles are of course developed, but these lie for the most part above the hand in the forearm. Those of the thenar and hypothenar eminences are somewhat larger and more square. Chiefly, the joints become enlarged, square and rugged and irregular in appearance. The tendons are more in evidence. The skin is hardened, so that creases are deeper; especially are the skin pads heavier and may overhang the borders. The skin hairs may stand up like bristles. In repose it assumes a more crooked position. Clenched, with the aggressive thumb twisted around the fingers, it becomes a squared, knobbed and formidable looking weapon.

The converse of this is true in the hand not inured to labor. The muscles of the palm present a softly rounded appearance, the skin is smooth and silky, the skin pads not clearly demarked; the joints are not only not rugged, but may be unduly flexible, small and weakly angled. The bones of the hand and fingers will have less of the spring curve, that is, will be straighter, and slighter. The hand will on the whole be much more symmetrical and expressionless.

When the hand is employed in what may by contrast be called the intelligent uses, in which flexibility is necessary, it will have as a consequence greater freedom of movement, will assume much more varied positions, and will express much more readily the mental states. In proportion as this habitual exercise is free and intelligent, will the symmetries assumed be free and expressive.

Certain typical positions are due not so much to the mental states as to the mechanics of the hand. For instance, the little finger side is always more flexible than the thumb side, because it is opposite to the powerful thumb. The middle finger is always inclined to bend farther forward, or to bend forward first; this on account of its relatively greater power. All fingers bend forward first at the knuckles, then at each joint in turn. The thumb is habitually carried somewhat extended, out of the way of the fingers.

Modern psychology, studying the dynamics of the nervous system, informs us in regard to many of the instinctive positions and actions of the body (including the hand) and the things expressed by them. For instance, there is a wholly involuntary opening out movement of the whole body, limbs and features, in pleasant emotions, honesty, courage, understanding, etc.; and conversely, there is a closing up, a drawing in, a turning away, in unpleasant emotions, in mental dishonesty, etc.

In states of self-consciousness, and the effort at self-control, there is a tendency to express the same by clasping one's self; as clasping the thumb with the fingers; clasping or twisting the other hand, or some part of the body.

THE HAND
Back View

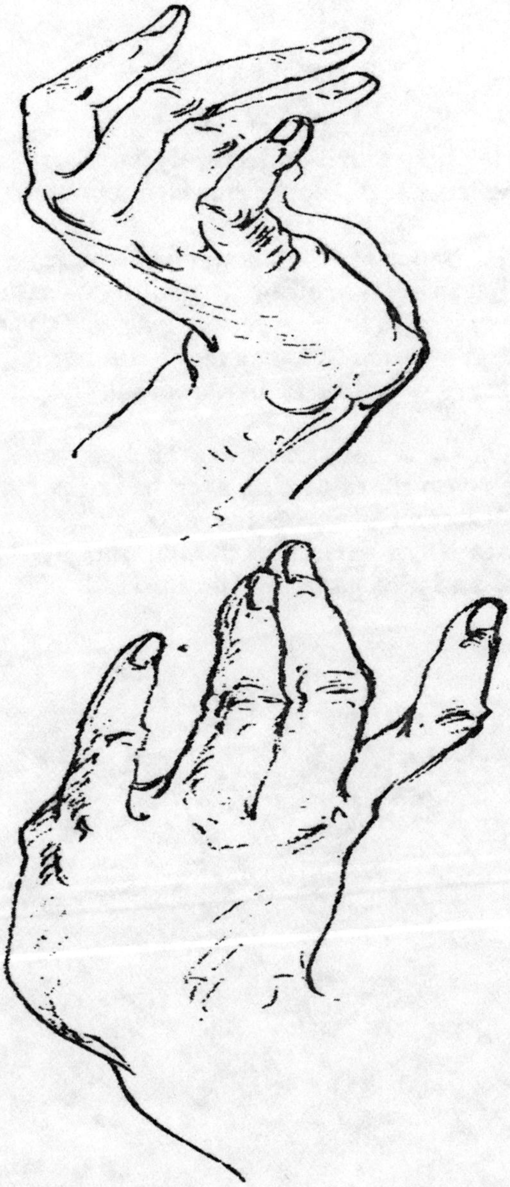

THE HAND

BACK VIEW

The wrist bones are collectively smaller than the end of the forearm, so there is a constriction at the sides.

The wrist bones are in two transverse layers with an angle between, forming in profile view a hook, point backward (mechanisms, page 159): over which is a step-down to the back of the hand. A little to the outer side, this is bridged by the extensor tendons.

The rows of wrist bones are arched toward the back. The two pillars of this arch in front far overhang the anterior line of the arm (pages 33, 39, 163). From them arise the thenar and hypothenar eminences, and the palm of the hand.

THE HAND

Back View

Except for the thumb and the extensor tendons, the back of the hand is smooth. It is slightly arched from side to side.

It is beveled from knuckles to wrist, and is narrower on the back than on the palmar surface. There is a slight fan-like movement among the bones of the hand.

The general mass of the back flows from the wrist toward the first and second knuckles, and is flattened and thinned toward the little finger side.

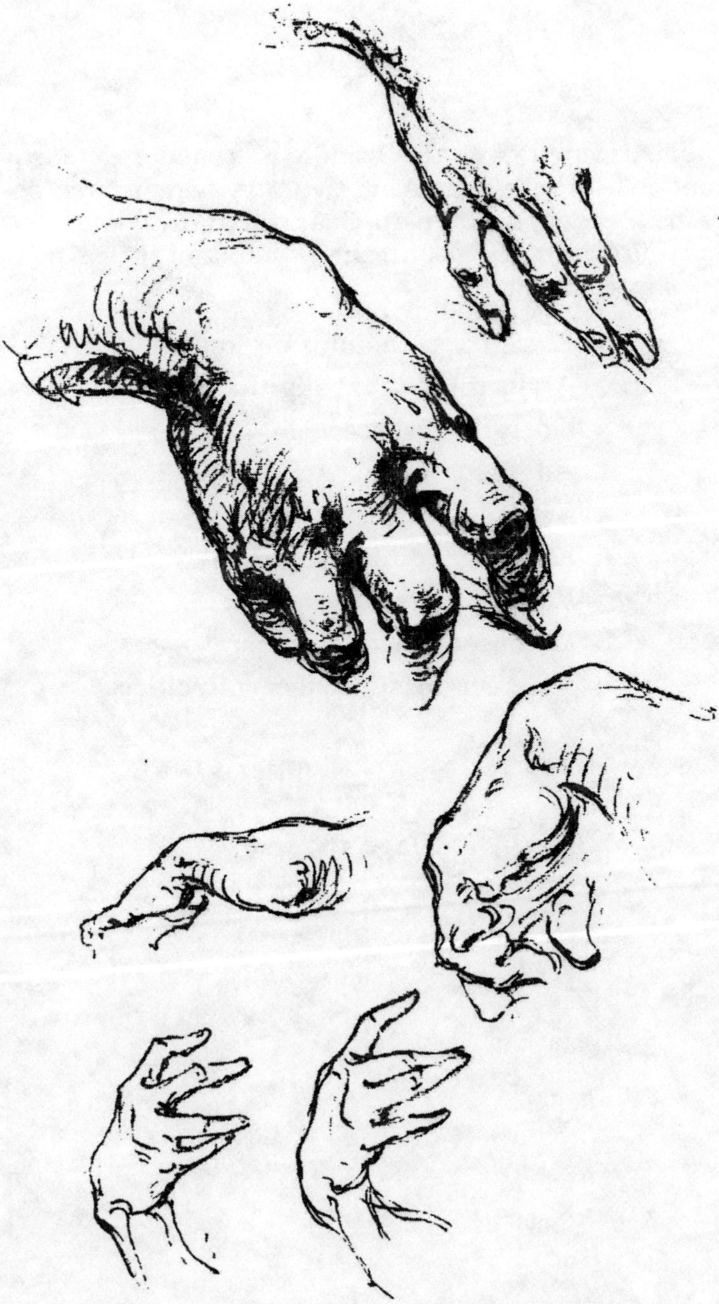

THE HAND

Back View

Distributed over the back are seen the extensor tendons. These represent two sets which have become blended, so have duplications and various connecting bands. Those to the thumb and little finger remain separate.

1 Extensor communis digitorum.
2 Abductor minimi digiti.
3 Dorsal interosseous.
4 Adductor pollicis.
5 Extensor carpi ulnaris.
6 Extensor minimi digiti.
7 Extensor longus pollicis.
8 Extensor brevis pollicis.
9 Extensor ossis metacarpi pollicis.

Origin, Insertion and Action of Muscles
Page 169

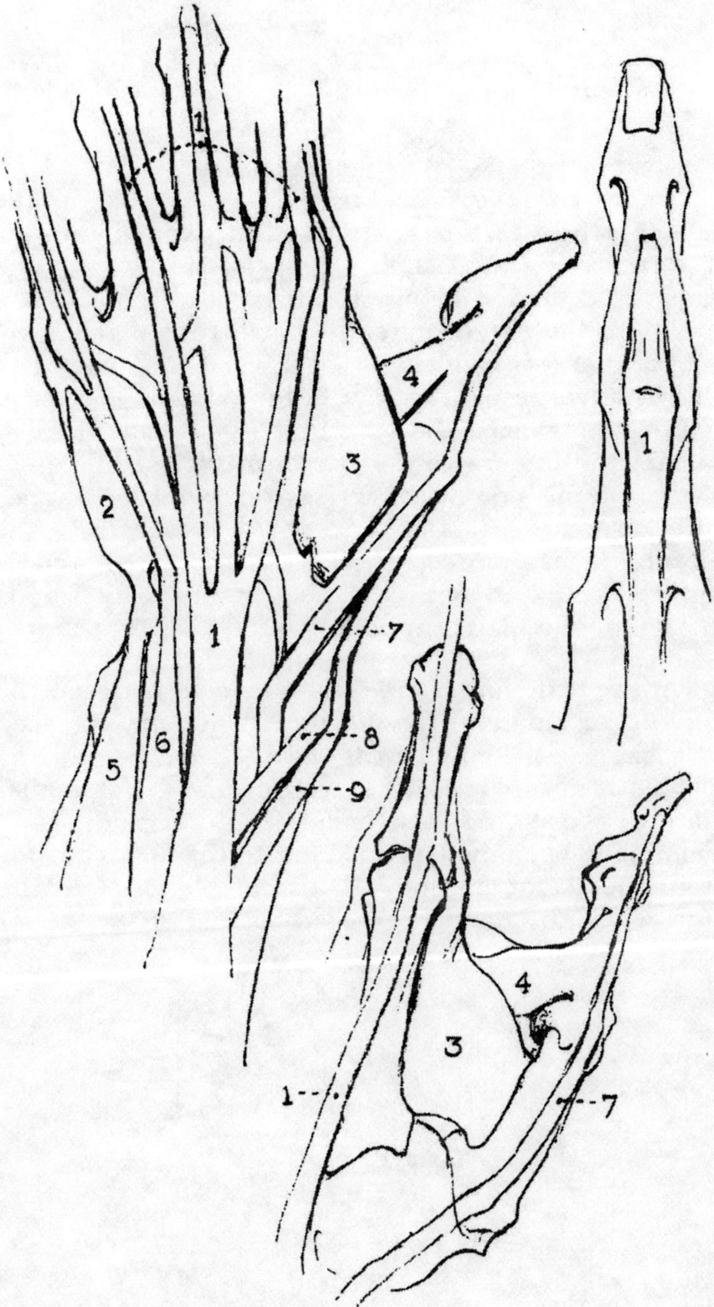
1
2
3
4
1
5
6
7
8
9
1
1
3
4
7

THE HAND

Back View

Unlike those of the front, the tendons on the back of the hand pass quite high over the wrist. It is clearly impossible to arch the wrist both ways; and flexion being so much more important a function, the extensor tendons are forced far from the centre of movement backward and outward. They converge on the low outer part of the wrist arch. Thus placed they are taut in extreme flexion, so that the fingers cannot be tightly closed.

The thumb side of the wrist arch is larger, higher and projects farther forward, carrying the thumb; it has a deeper inset at the wrist and is square compared with the heel inside, which ends in a ball—the pisiform bone.

On the little finger side of the wrist, between the end of the ulna and the pisiform bone, may be seen a "rocker"—the cuneiform bone.

This is the part of the arch of the wrist immediately above the pisiform—its outer end. It is prominent when the hand is bent to the opposite side or in the act of pulling. It almost blends with the ulna when the hand is carried to that side.

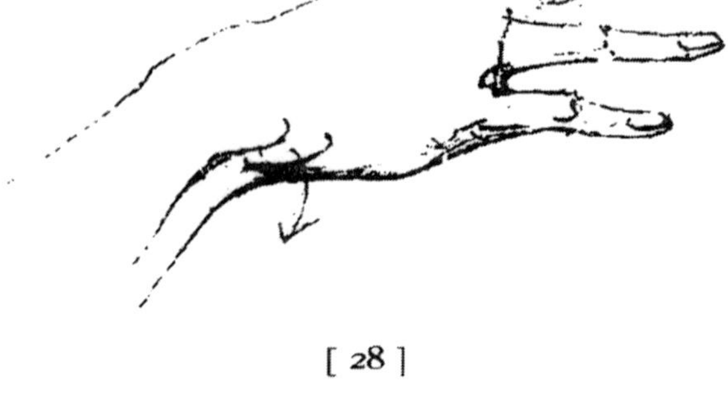

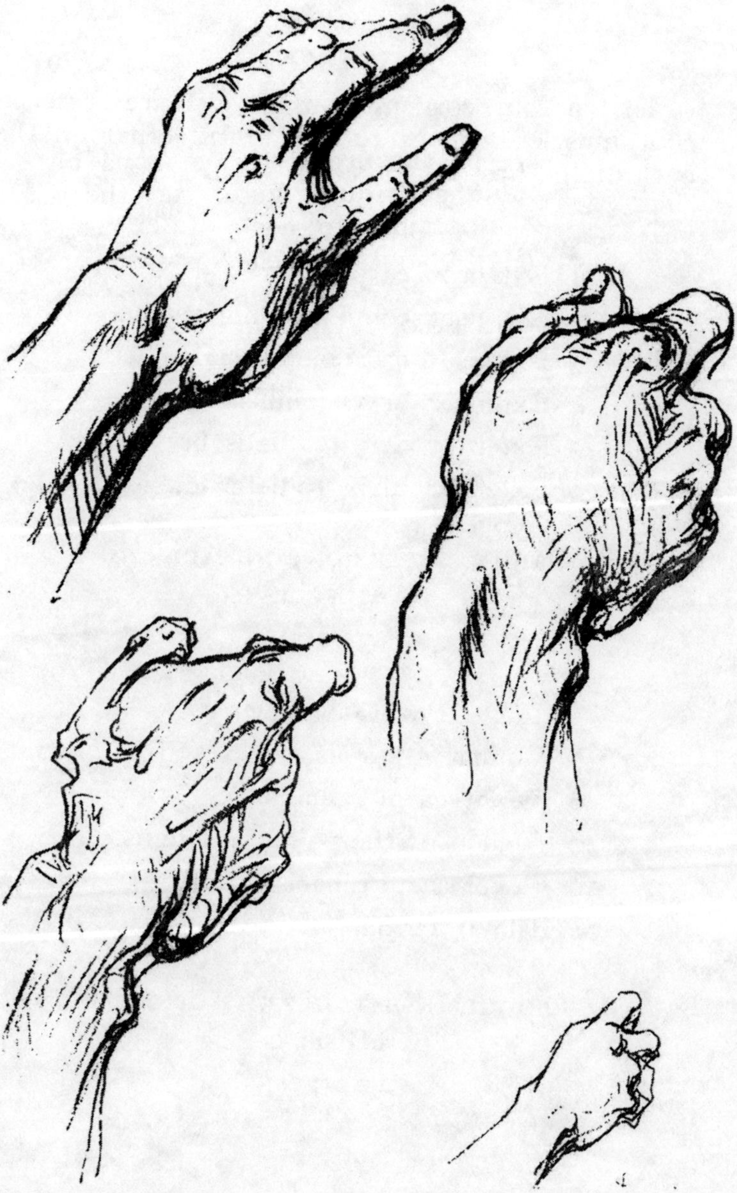

THE HAND

To the four corners of the wrist are fastened four muscles, one of them doubled (that on the back of the first finger side).

Back View

1 Extensor carpi ulnaris.

2 Extensor communis digitorum.

3 Extensor ossis metacarpi pollicis.

4 Extensor brevis pollicis.

5 Extensor carpi radialis brevior.

6 Extensor carpi radialis longior.

Origin, Insertion and Action of Muscles
Page 169

Palmar View

7 Supinator longus.

8 Flexor carpi radialis.

9 Tendon of the palmaris longus.

10 Flexor carpi ulnaris.

11 Palmar fascia.

Origin, Insertion and Action of Muscles
Page 171

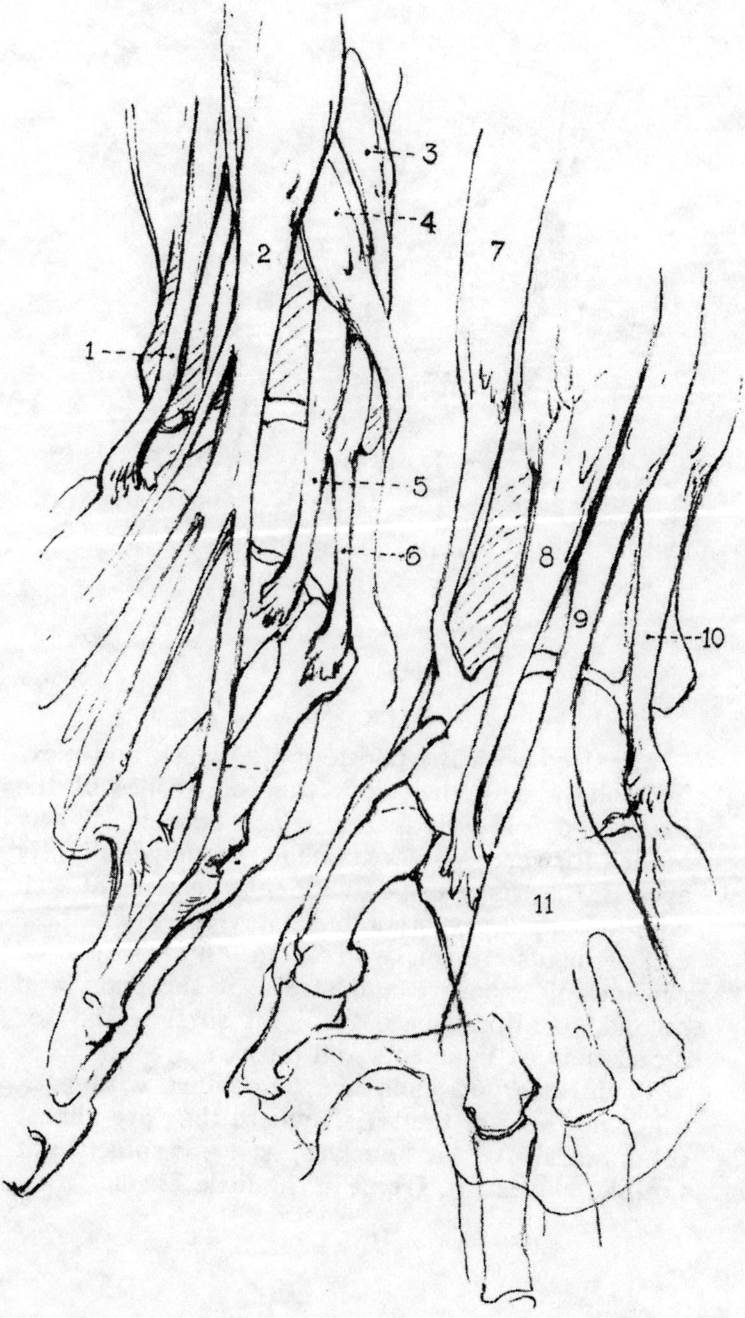

1
2
3
4
5
6
7
8
9
10
11

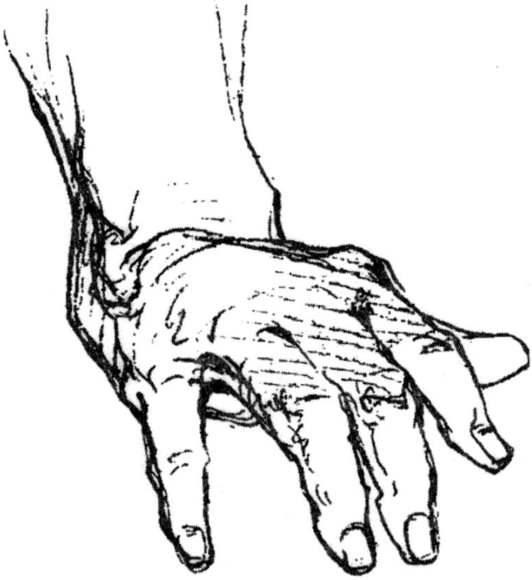

THE HAND

Back View

Morticed with the bones of the wrist, and moving solidly with them, are the four bones of the hand, one for each finger. Each bone is slightly arched forward, as every bone in the body is slightly arched; they have a shaft with enlargements at each end, also as every other bone in the body. These enlargements are for two reasons—first, safety, on account of exposure and strain at the ends, and second, to afford space for joint surface and for attachment of ligaments and muscles.

Their enlarged ends are in contact with each other not only at the wrist, where they are almost solid, but also at the knuckles, where is some slight fan-like movement, freest in the little finger.

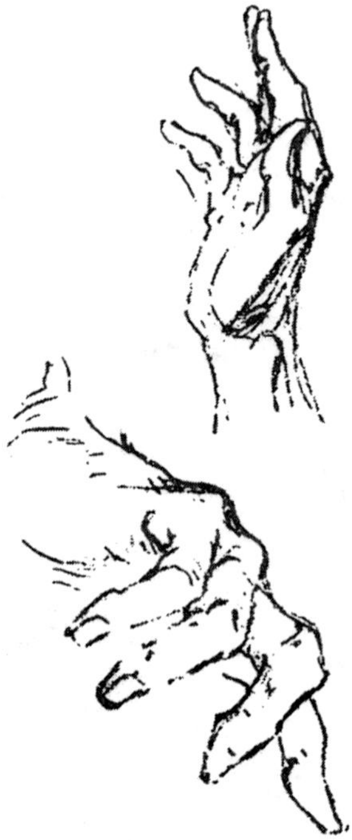

THE HAND

Back View

The hand is arched backward from side to side, being highest at the second finger.

The arch reaches from the metacarpal bone of the first finger to that of the little finger.

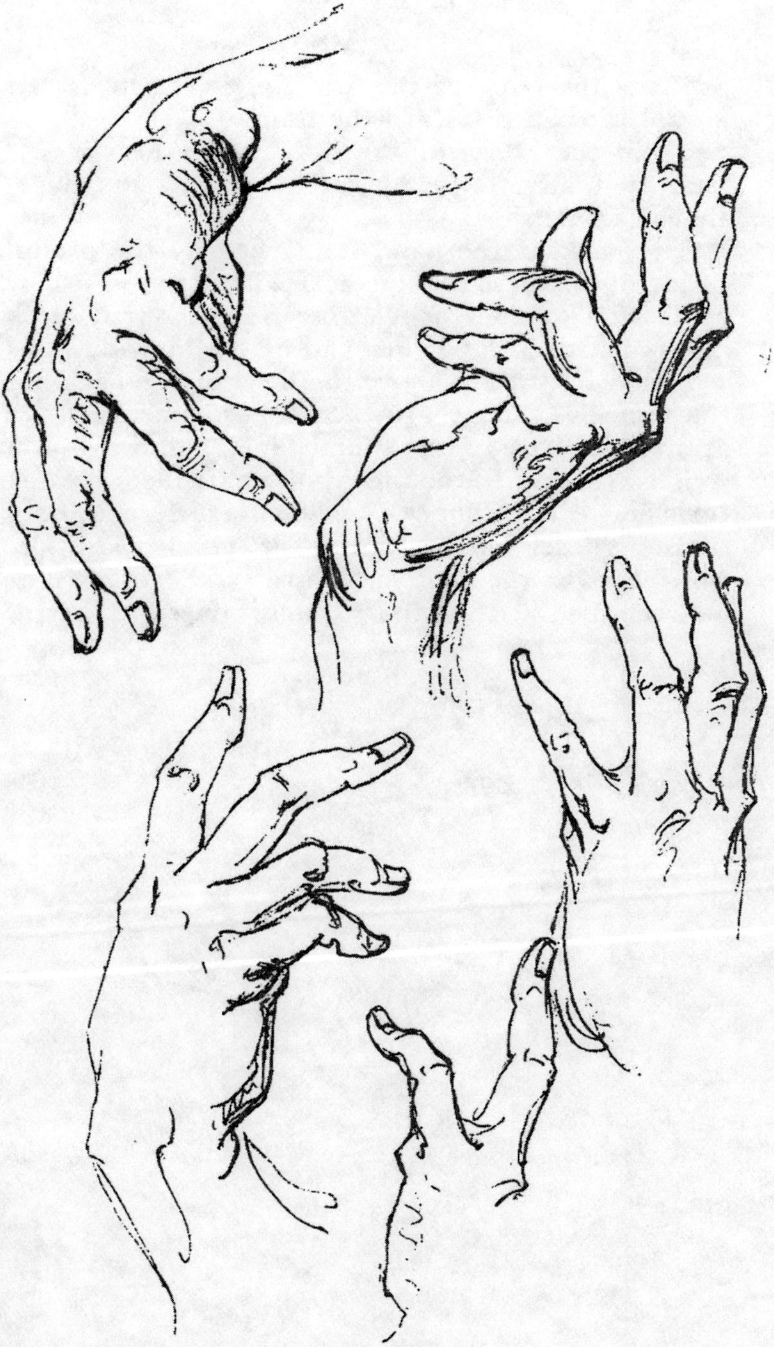

THE HAND

Back View

From the bone of the first finger the mass sets sharply forward toward the thumb.

From the bones of the little finger also it sets sharply forward, forming the back of the hypothenar eminence.

The back of the hand is marked by the prominence of the first two metacarpals at the wrist, by superficial tendons converging on the wrist, often covered with heavy veins, and by the knuckles.

Somewhat raised above the level of the back are the knuckles. They are in a curved line, concave around the base of the thumb; i. e., palmward and wristward. When the fingers are extended, creases form between the knuckles following different directions. These diverge from the middle knuckle, curving over the first and third, while that from between the third and fourth curves over the fourth.

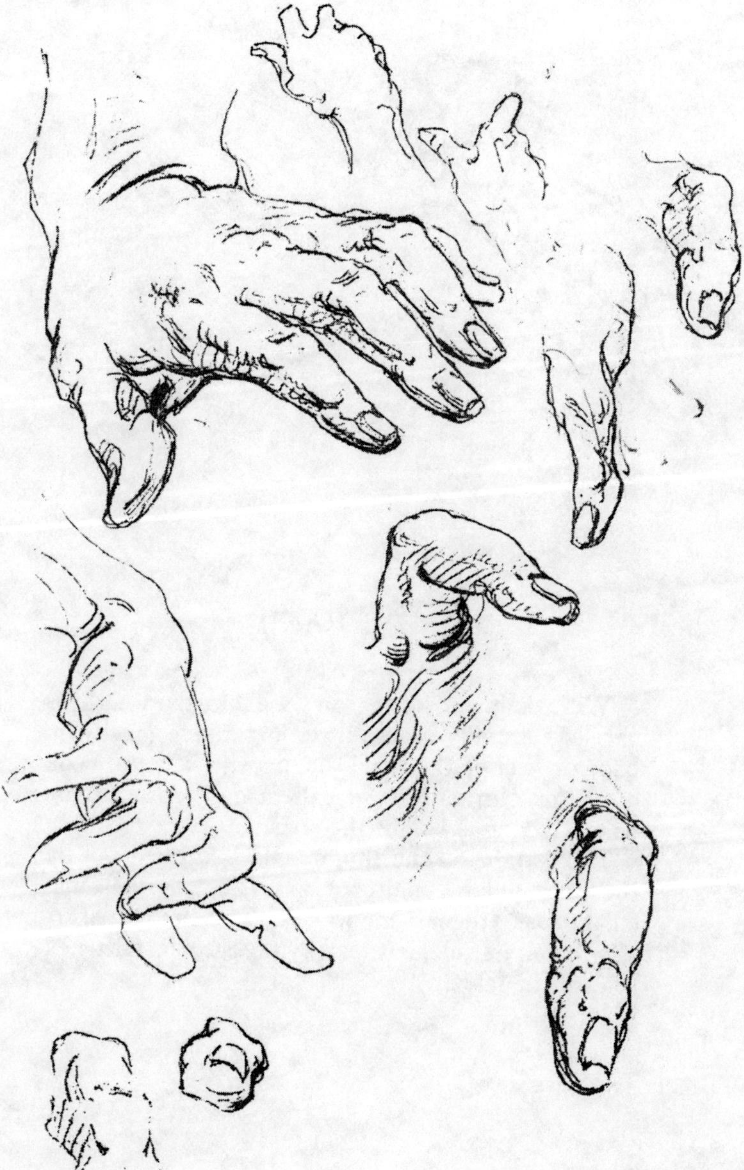

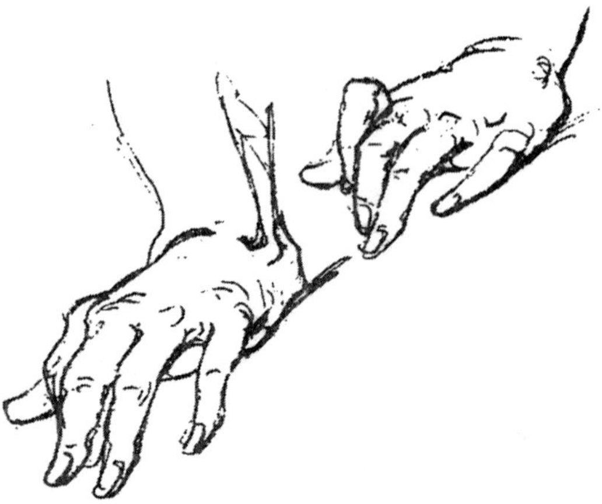

THE HAND

Back View

With the palm resting on the table, the weight is carried normally by the little finger side (pisiform bone or heel of the hand). Opposite it is the hook of the unciform. Between them the tendon of the palmaris longus bulges the wrist.

The weight on the thumb side is carried not by the wrist pillar (unciform bone), but by the muscular mass (thenar eminence). The thumb naturally lies on its side, but may by pressure be flattened toward the table.

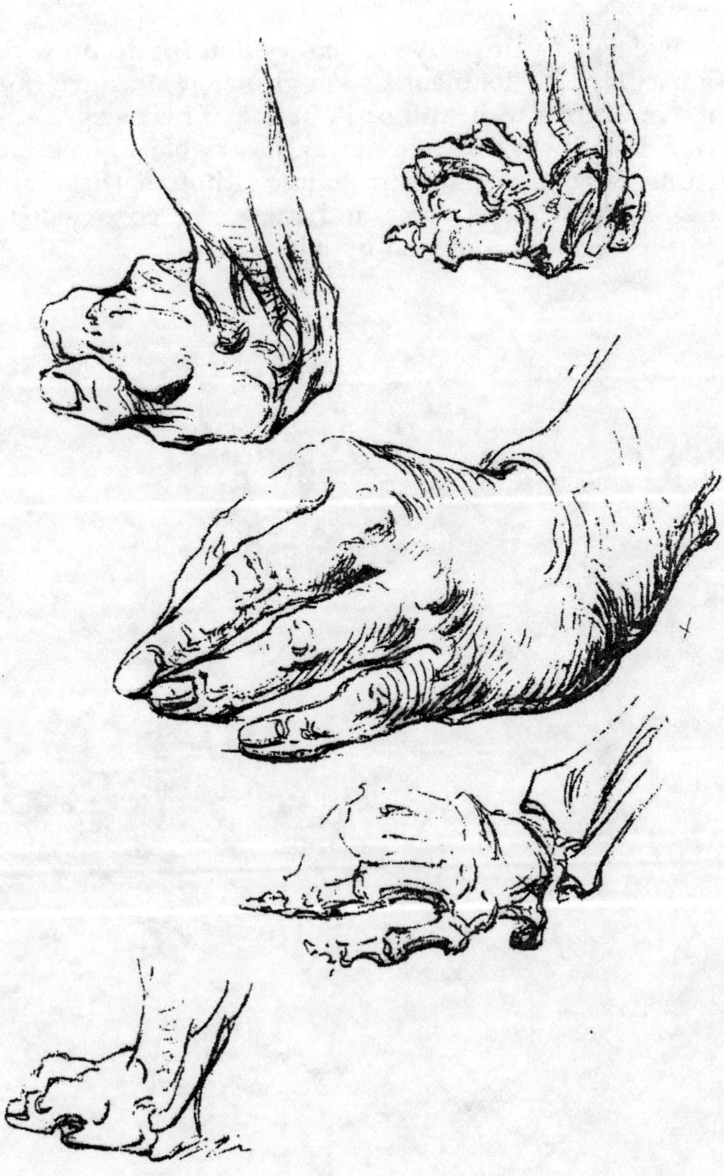

VEINS

Enlarged veins have in reality nothing to do with muscular development or rough usage, but are due to conditions of health or ill health. Their size, location and elevation are extremely variable. The same thing is true of the skin hairs, although these are more likely to be erect and therefore conspicuous in the hands roughened by labor.

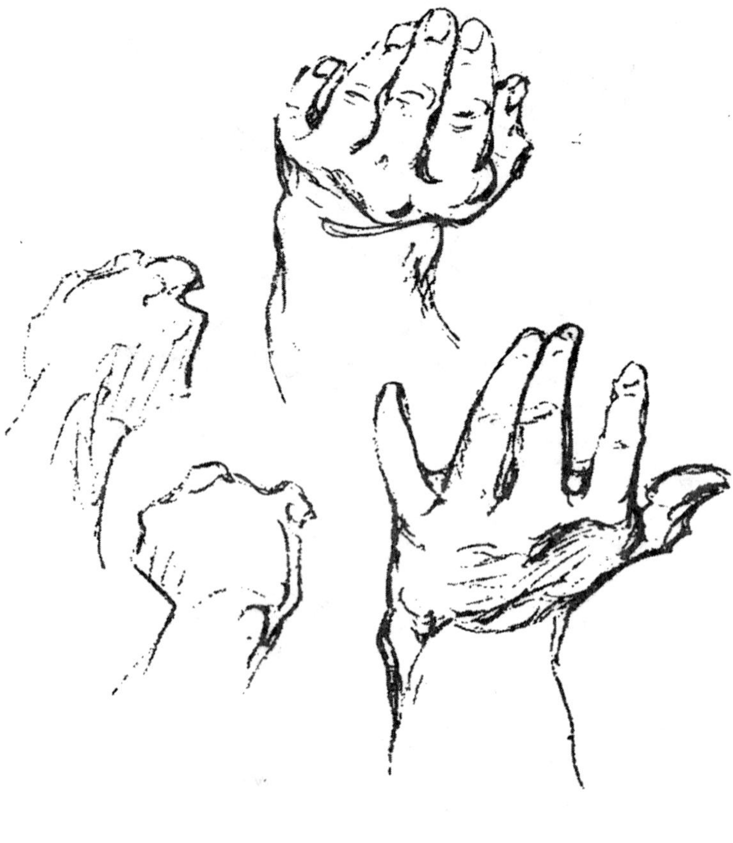

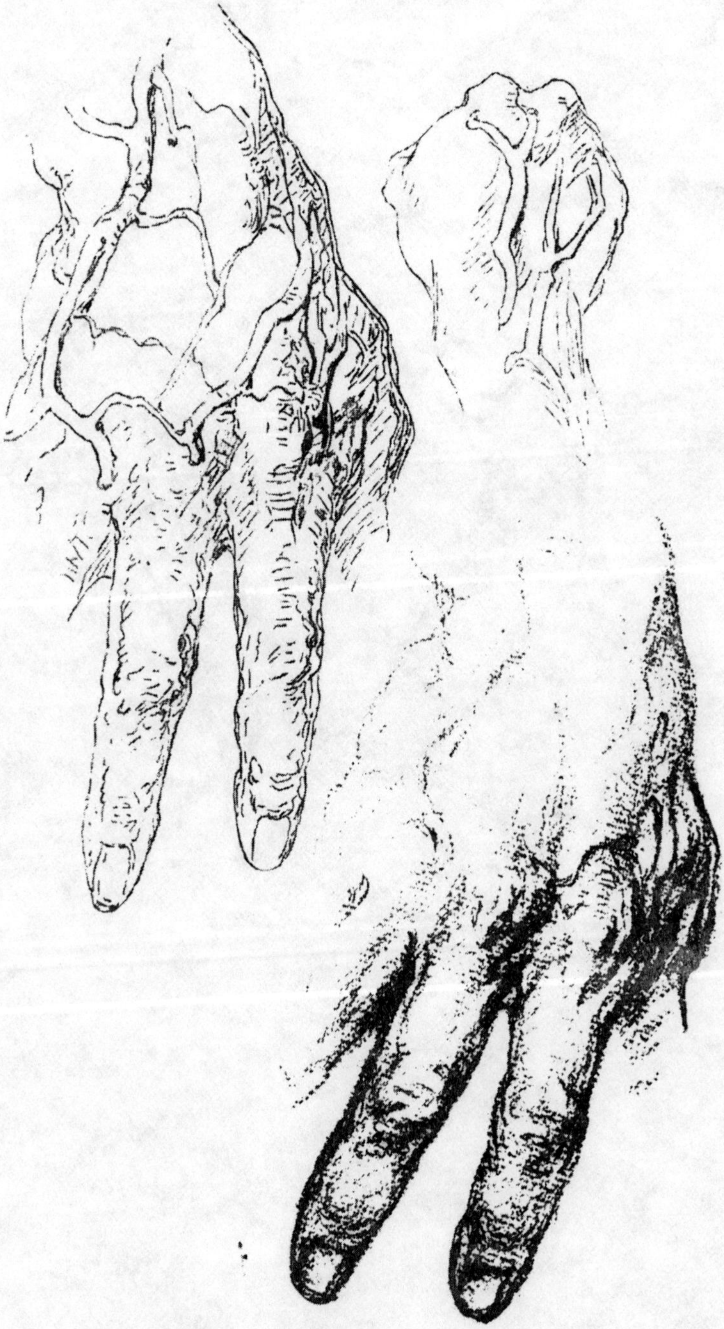

THE HAND

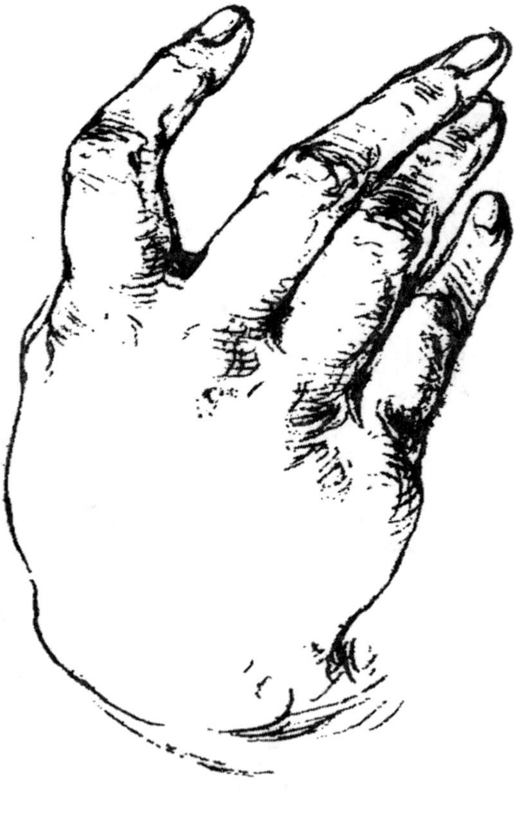

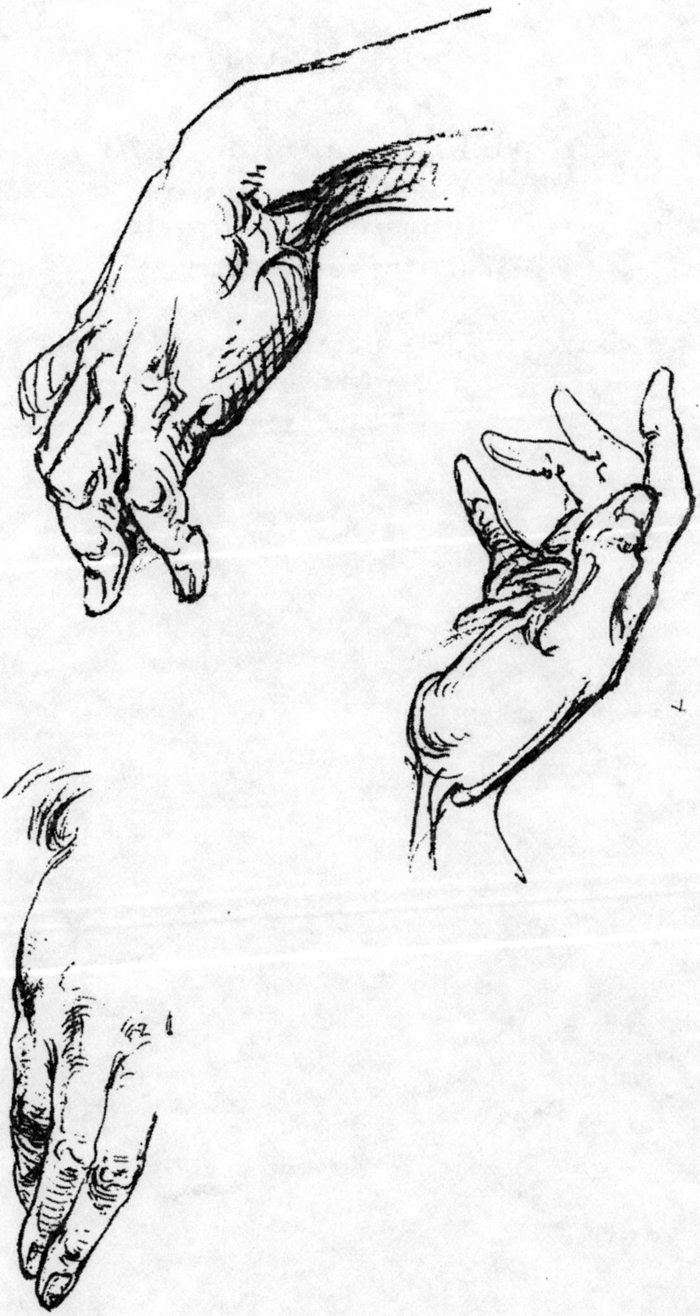

THE HAND

Back View

1 Abductor minimi digiti.

2 Tendons of extensor communis digitorum.

3 First dorsal interossei.

Origin, Insertion and Action of Muscles

Page 169

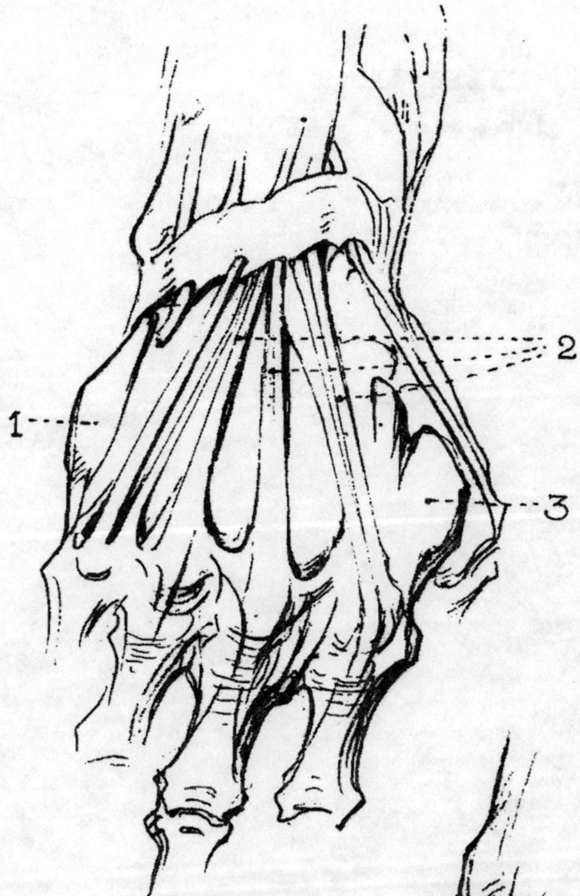
1
2
3

THE HAND
PALMAR VIEW

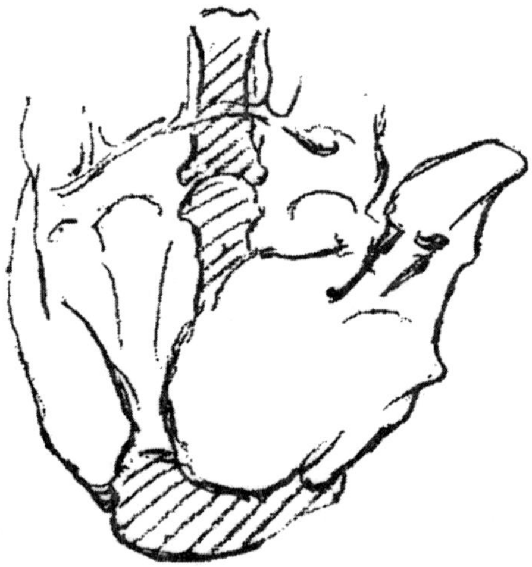

THE HAND

Palmar View

The palm slightly overlies the wrist, and extends to the middle of the first joint of the fingers. It is made of three portions, with the hollow of the palm between them.

On the thumb side is the largest of these portions, the thenar eminence; opposite it is the hypothenar eminence, and across under the knuckles is the third portion, the mounds of the palm.

The thenar eminence is high, fat and soft; it contains the short muscles of the thumb and forms with the bone the pyramidal first segment of it.

The hypothenar eminence is longer, lower, harder and more triangular. It contains some muscles of the little finger, large on account of the exposed position of that digit, and part of the palmaris brevis. It reaches as far as the base of the little finger, blending there with the row of mounds. At the wrist it covers the pisiform bone, with a heavy fibrous pad like that of the heel.

The bones as a group form a mass that is beveled from wrist to fingers, and from thumb to little finger side, in profile; and in palmar or dorsal view, from knuckles to wrist. The mass is slightly concave forward, following the curve of the wrist.

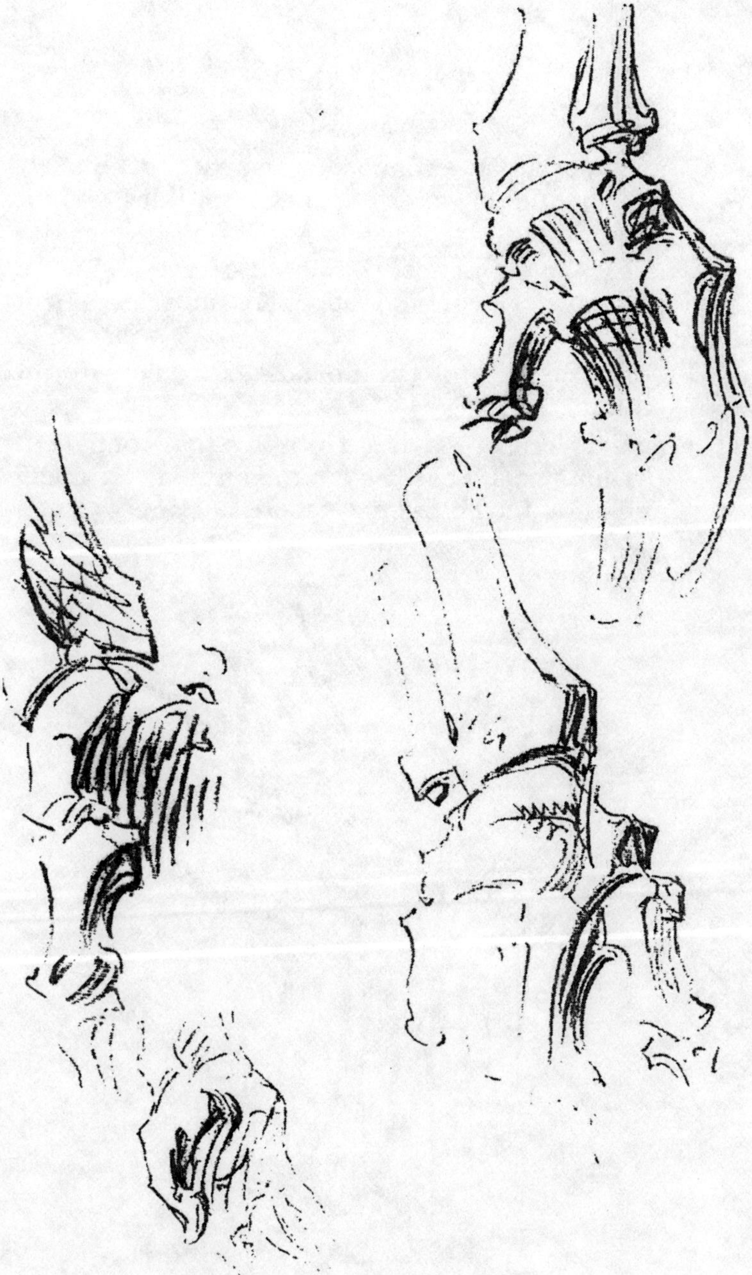

THE HAND

Palmar View

1 The hypothenar eminence, composed of the abductor, flexor and opponens muscles of the little finger.

2 The thenar eminence, composed of the abductor, adductor, flexor and opponens muscles of the thumb.

3 Palmar fascia and the fibrous expansion of the palm.

4 Palmaris longus—arises from internal condyle of the humerus, passes over the annular ligament and ends in the palmar fascia. (Page 55)

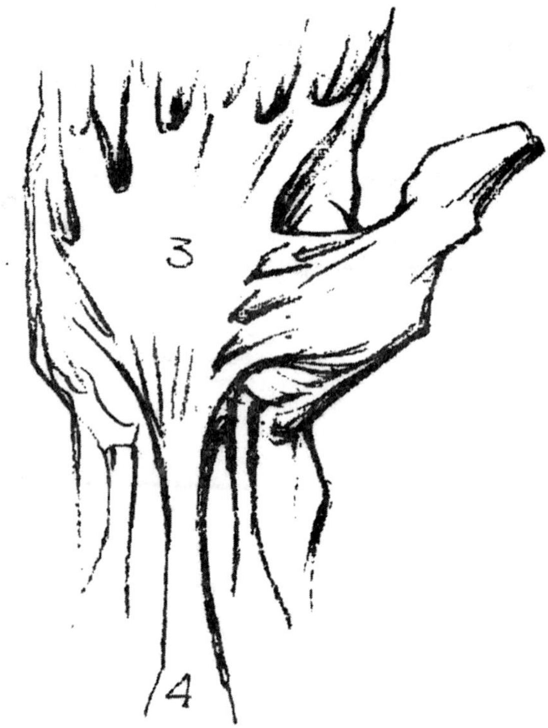

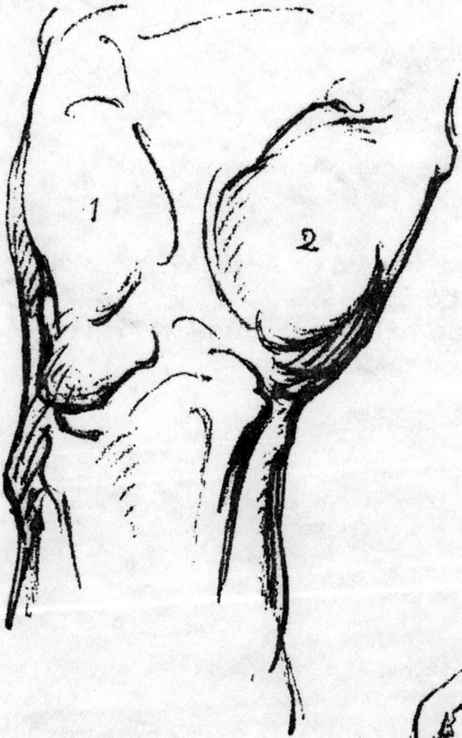
1
2

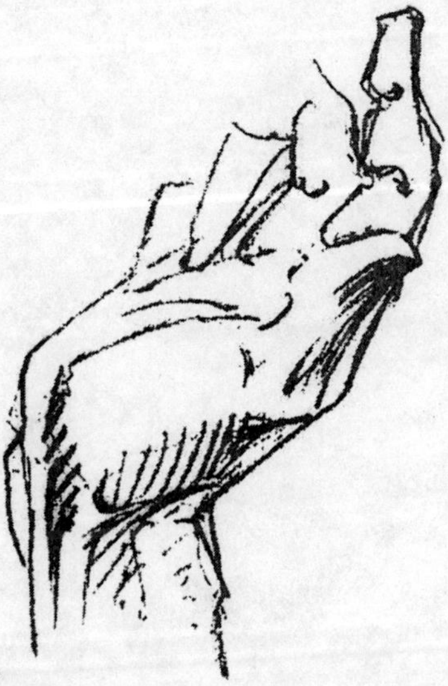

THE HAND

Palmar View

The mounds of the palm are beyond the line of knuckles on the back, lying over the enlarged ends of the first phalanges.

They are flattened, bulged or wrinkled, according to the position of the fingers.

The hollow of the palm is triangular, traversed by the tendon of the middle finger.

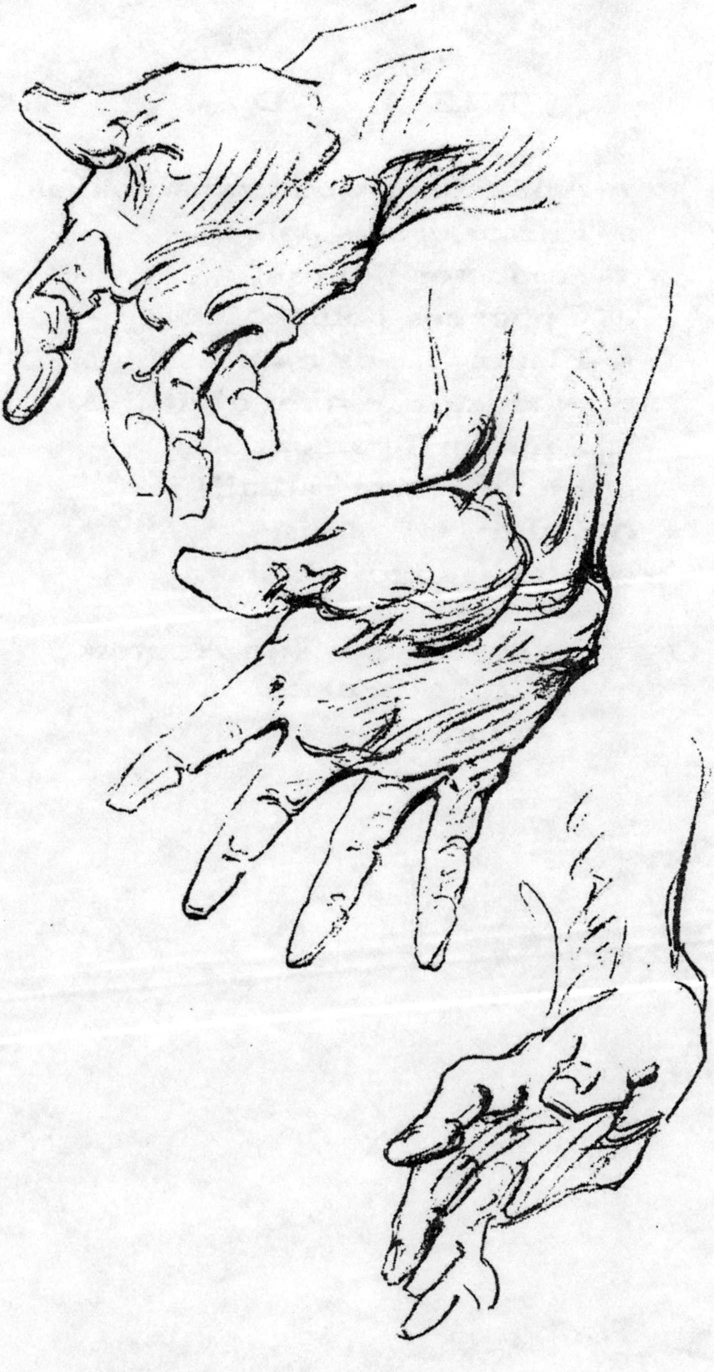

THE HAND

Palmar View

1 Adductor transversus pollicis.
2 Flexor brevis pollicis.
3 Abductor pollicis.
4 Opponens pollicis.
5 Flexor brevis minimi digiti.
6 Abductor minimi digiti.
7 Annular ligament.
8 Flexor carpi radialis.
9 Palmaris longus.
10 Flexor carpi ulnaris.

Origin, Insertion and Action of Muscles
Pages 169-171

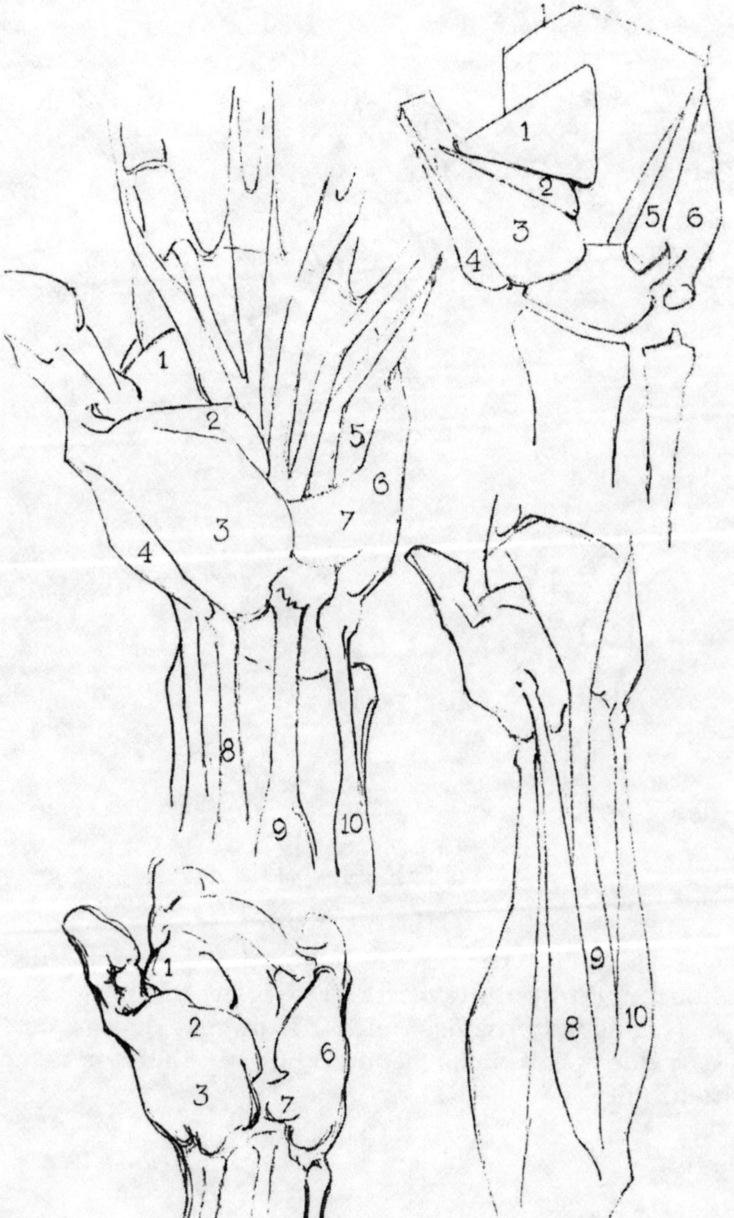
1
2
3
4
5
6
7
8
9
10
1
2
3
4
5
6
8
9
10
1
2
3
6
7

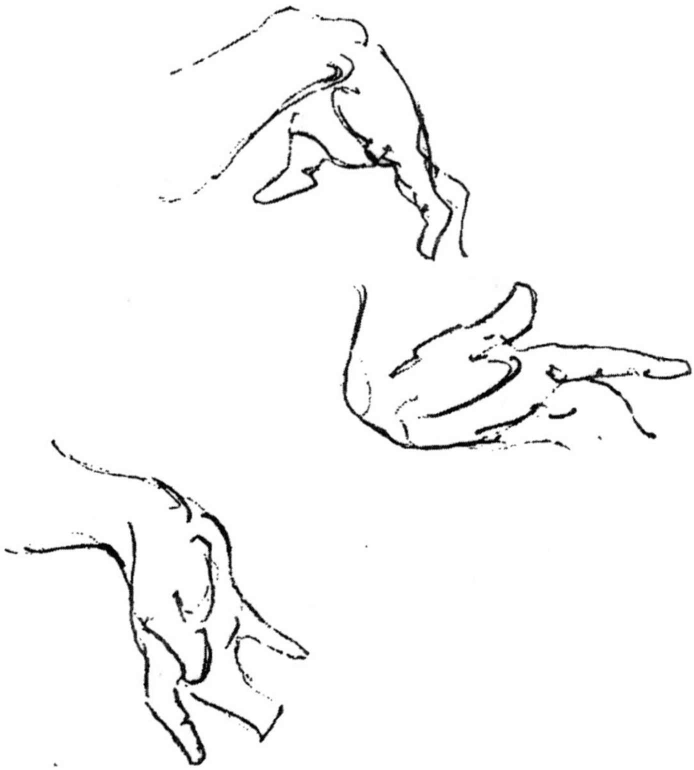

THE HAND

PALMAR VIEW

It is usually the middle finger that is found most hooked, on account of its greater strength.

It is usually the first and little fingers that assume extreme positions, on account of their greater flexibility.

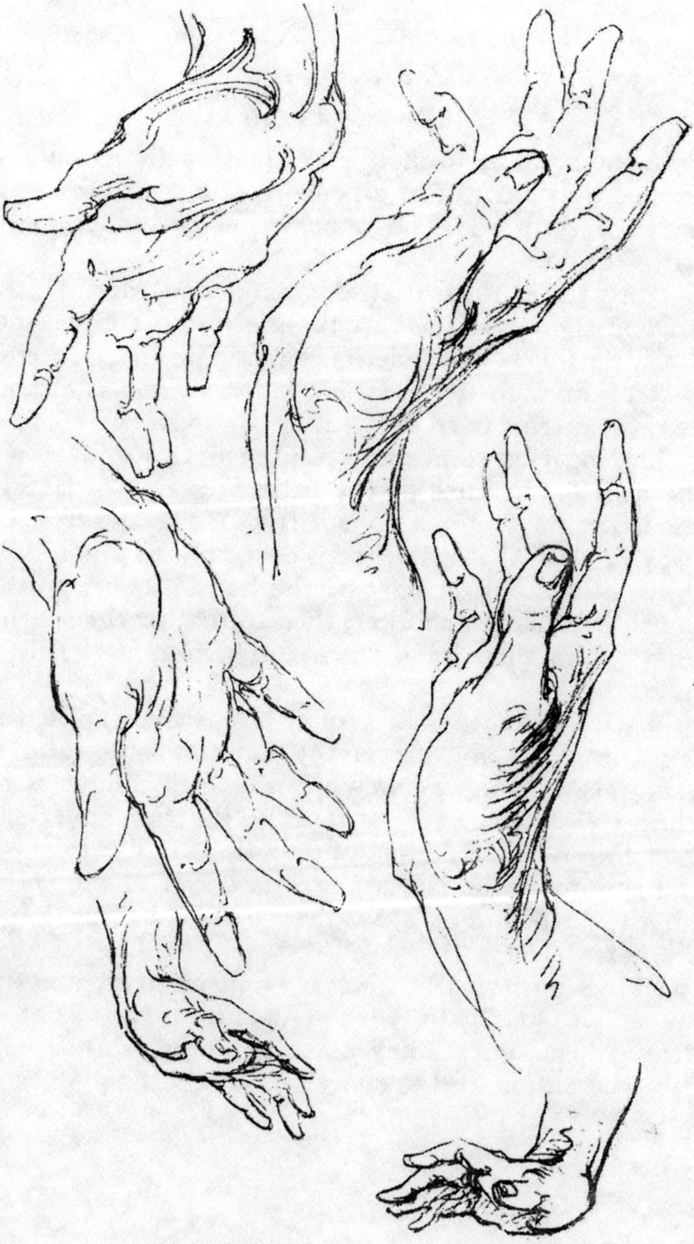

THE HAND

PALMAR VIEW

CONSTRUCTION

In the hand as in the figure there is an action and an inaction side. The side with the greatest angle is the action side, the opposite is the inaction or straight side.

With the hand turned down (prone) and drawn toward the body, the thumb side is the action side, the little finger the inaction side. The inaction side is straight with the arm, while the thumb is almost at right angles with it.

The inaction construction line runs straight down the arm to the base of the little finger. The action construction line runs down the arm to the base of the thumb at the wrist, from there out to the middle joint, at the widest part of the hand; thence to the knuckle of the first finger, then to that of the second finger, and then joins the inaction line at the little finger.

With the hand still prone, but drawn *from* the body, the thumb side is the inaction side, and is straight with the arm, while the little finger is at almost right angles with it. The inaction construction line now runs straight to the middle joint of the thumb, while the action line runs to the wrist on the little finger side, thence to the first joint, etc., etc.

These construction lines, six in number, are the same with the palm turned up, according as it is drawn in or out. They place the fingers and indicate the action and proportions of the hand.

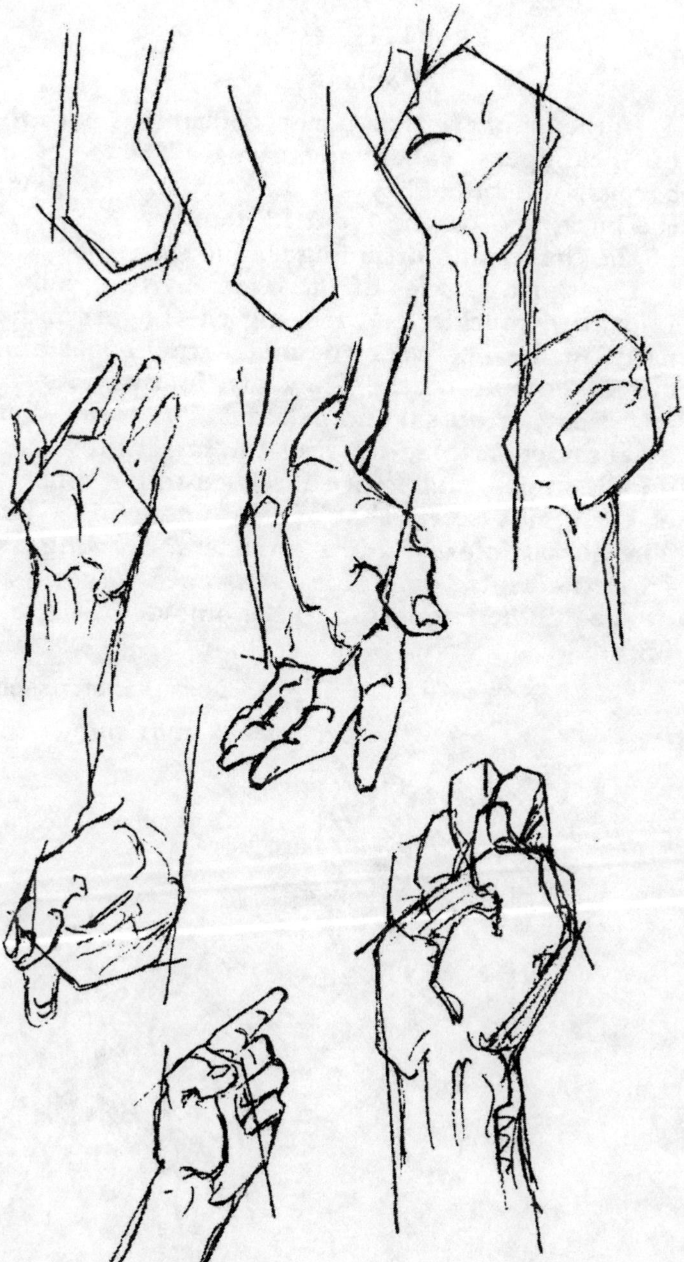

THE HAND

Palmar View

In the hand are four bones, continuous with those of the fingers, called metacarpals (*meta,* beyond, *carpus,* wrist). They are covered by tendons on the back, and on the front by tendons, the muscles of the thumb and little finger, and skin pads.

The short muscles of the hand, crossing only one joint, the knuckle, and moving the fingers individually, lie deep between the metacarpal bones and so are called interossei. They are in two sets, back and front, or dorsal and palmar. The palmar interossei are collectors, drawing the fingers toward the middle finger, and so are fastened to the inner side of each joint except that of the middle finger itself. The dorsal interossei are spreaders, drawing away from the centre, and so are fastened to both sides of the middle finger and to the outside of the other joints.

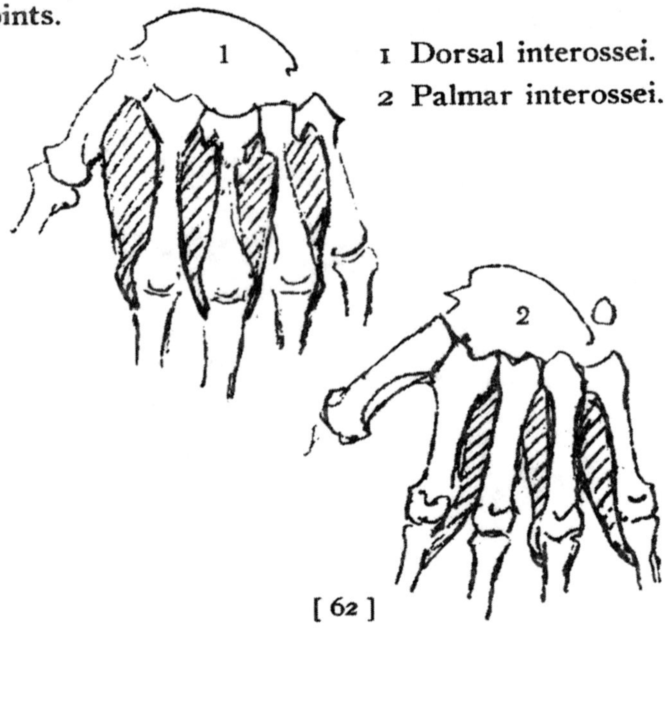

1 Dorsal interossei.

2 Palmar interossei.

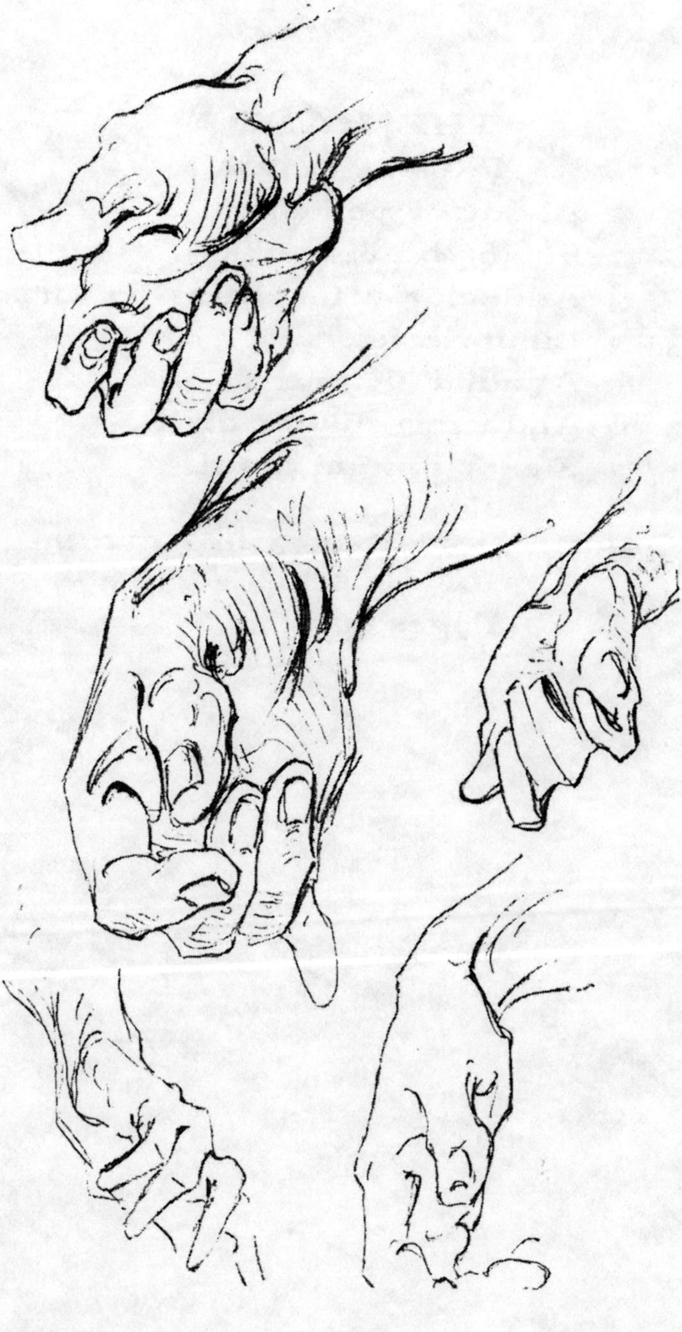

THE HAND

Palmar View

1 Abductor pollicis.
2 Flexor brevis pollicis.
3 Adductor transversus pollicis.
4 Lumbricales.
5 Annular ligament.
6 Abductor minimi digiti.
7 Flexor minimi digiti.

Origin, Insertion and Action of Muscles
Pages 169-171

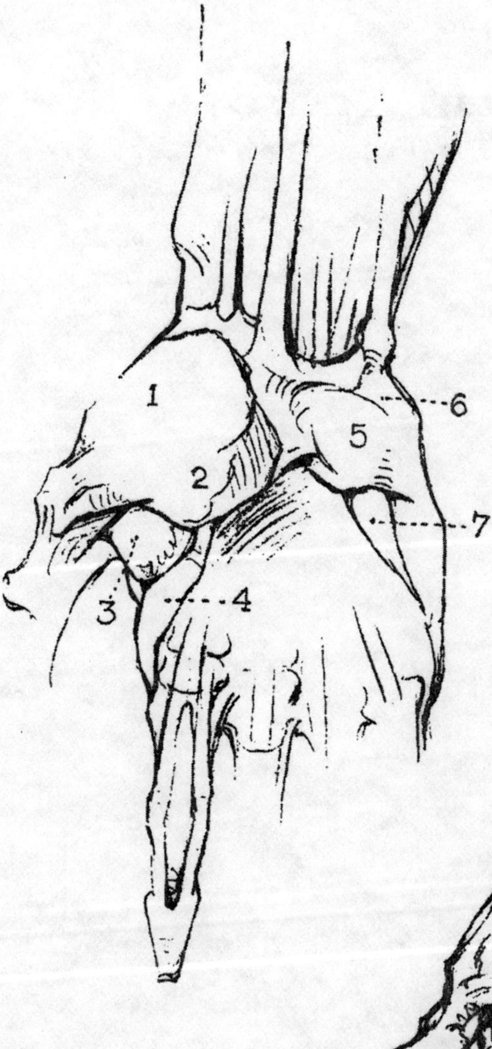
1
2
3
4
5
6
7

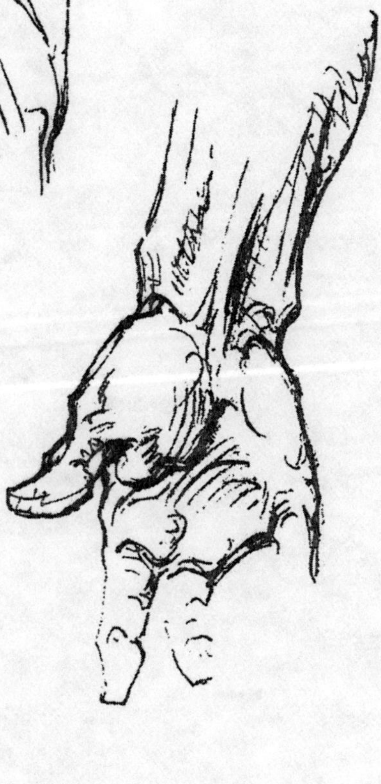

THE HAND
Thumb Side

THE HAND
Thumb Side

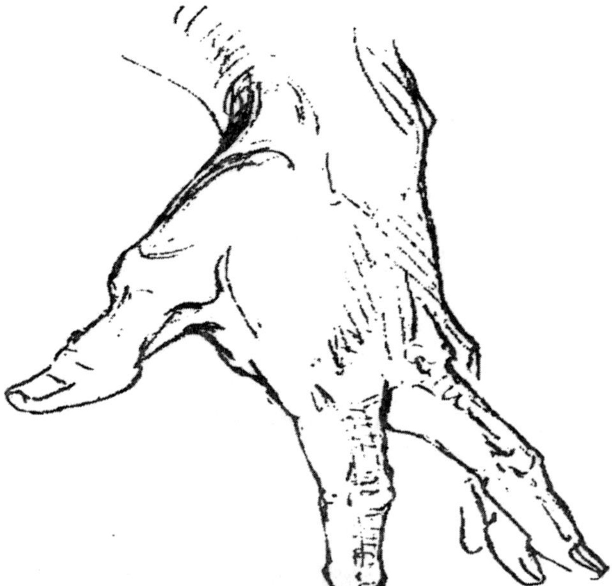

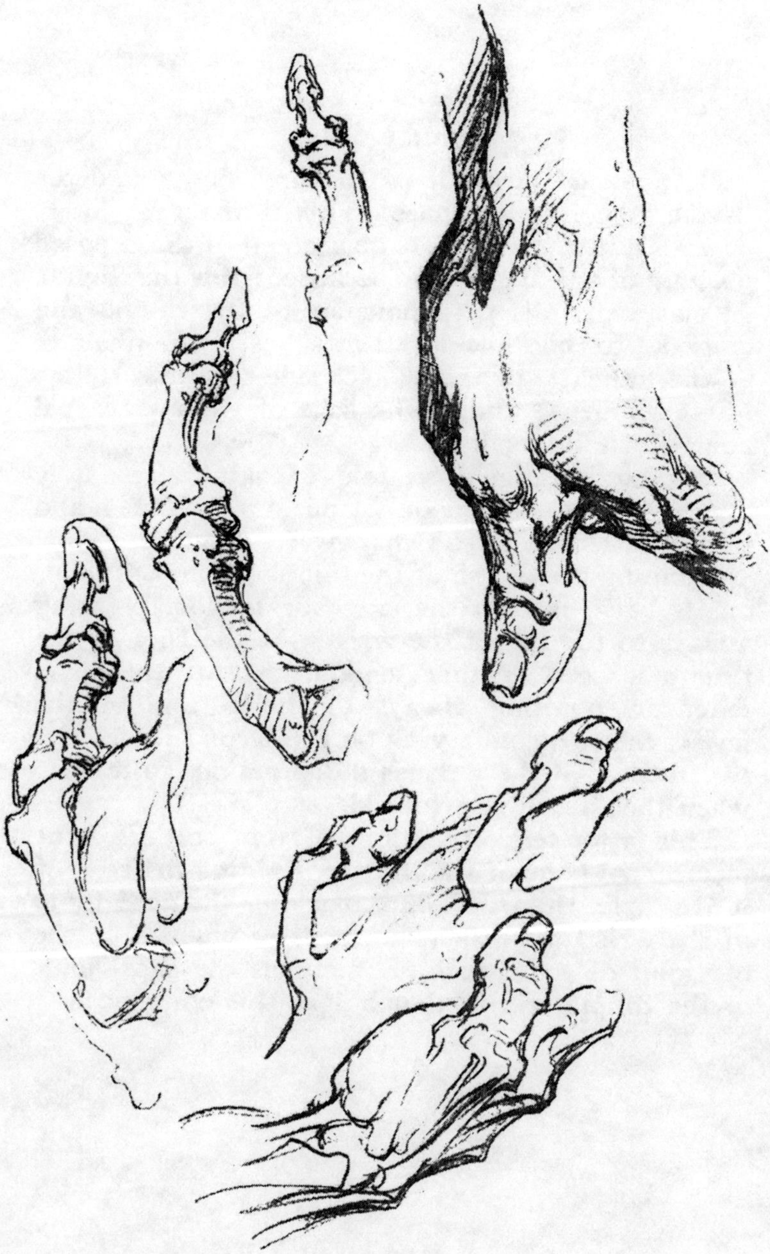

THE HAND

Thumb Side

Between the knuckle of the first finger and the thumb is a bulging mass. This is the first interosseous muscle, large here on account of the exposed position of the finger, also because it aids the thumb. In clasping, it is perpendicular to the thumb and diagonal to the knuckle. It attaches to the phalanx at the knuckle, to the whole side of the thumb (first segment) and to the base of the metacarpal bone of the finger itself.

Beyond its edge is a fold of skin; alternately drawn into a half-moon blade, and dimpled and wrinkled, as the thumb changes its position.

Running the length of the thumb to the last joint, on its back, is seen the extensor tendon, pointing always to the top of the wrist. At the root of the thumb is seen another tendon, that of the short extensor, pointing always to the bottom of the wrist; the two converging on the second joint. Between them at the wrist is a depression, quite deep when the thumb is extended.

This latter tendon marks the front border of the metacarpal bone of the thumb. Bulging in front of it are, first, the trapezium, marking the radial end of the wrist arch, then the thenar eminence, to the big joint of the thumb. Sometimes the basal joint of the thumb still farther bulges this eminence.

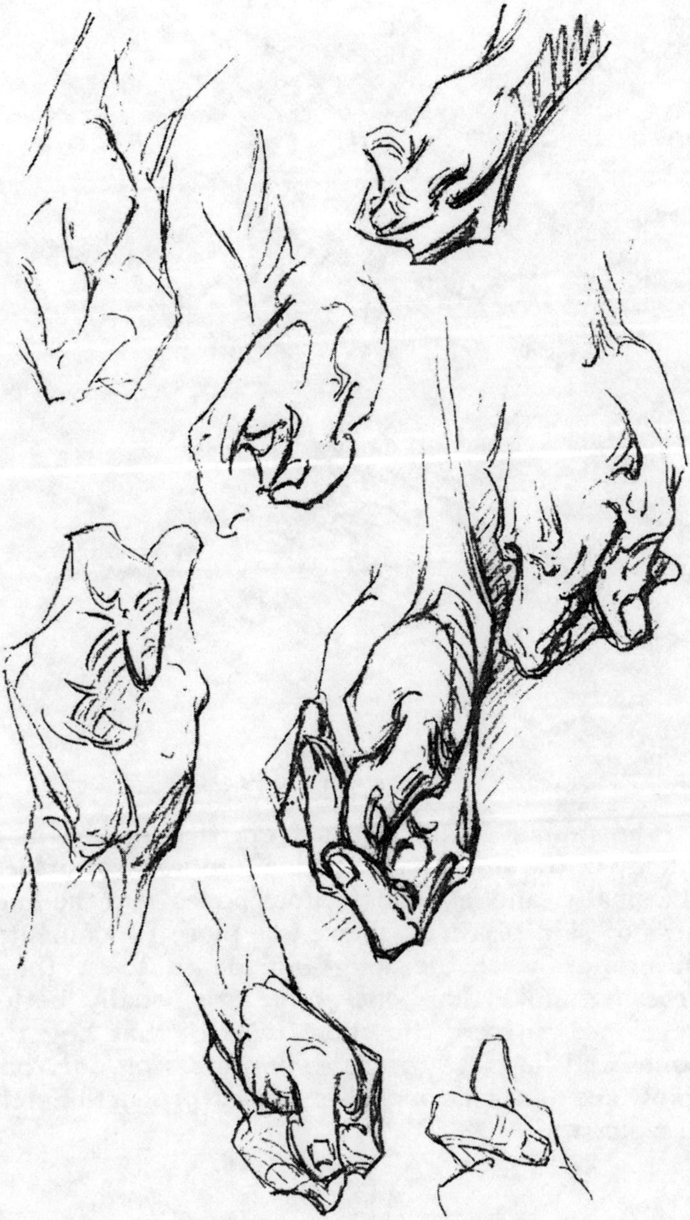

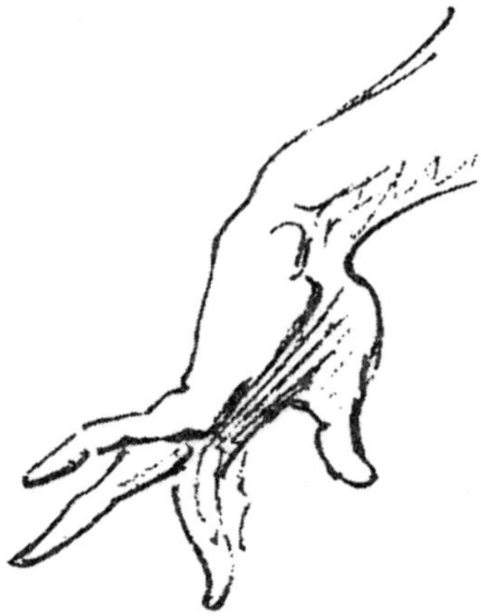

THE HAND

The female hand differs from that of the male chiefly in the smaller size of the joints and knuckles, the smaller and less conspicuous bones, and the fineness of skin texture. There is a more fundamental difference also: the long outside muscles, those crossing more than one joint, are usually better developed in men, the short muscles that hug the bones and lie close to the joints, crossing only one joint, are as a rule more developed proportionately in women.

THE HAND

Thumb Side

The mass of the hand sets at an angle across the end of the forearm; the mass of the thumb sets at an angle across the base of the hand.

The Muscles of the Thumb

1 Long extensor of the thumb.

2 Short extensor of the thumb.

3 Long abductor of the thumb.

Origin, Insertion and Action of Muscles

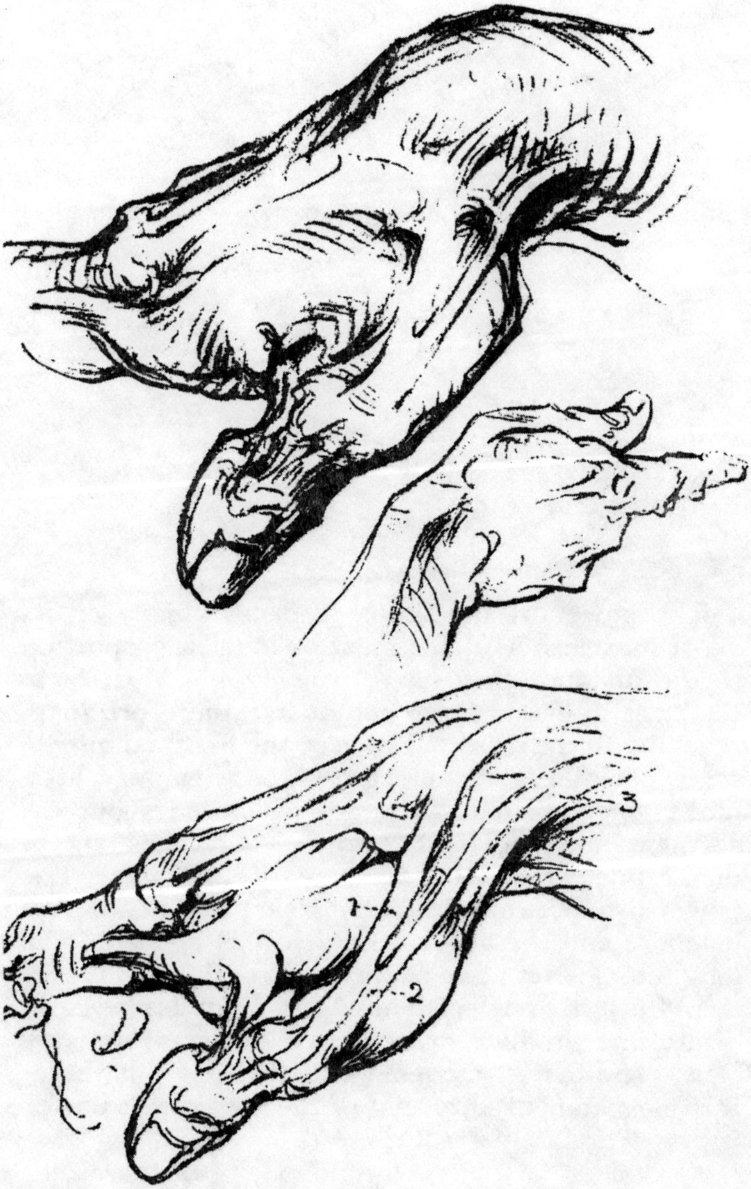
3
1
2

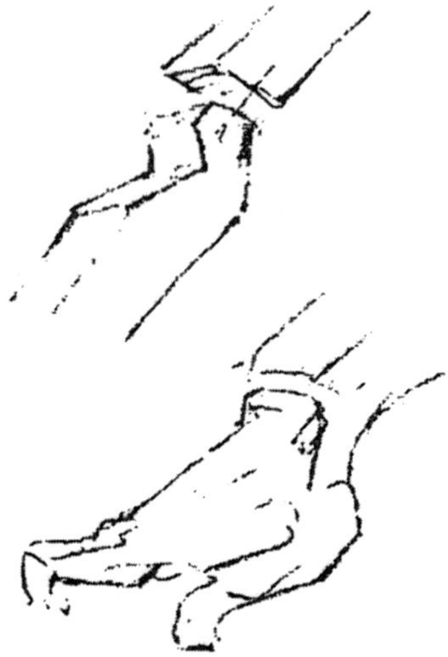

THE HAND

Thumb Side

The power of the thumb depends chiefly on its short muscles. Muscles must be long in proportion to the distance they have to contract. Muscles to the ends of fingers and thumb are therefore long, reaching to the elbow. Those of the first and middle segments of the thumb (the latter with very little movement) are short and are developed about the segment and across the palm, where they act in direct line with the movement of the bone. The power produced by muscular action depends on the leverage and the angle at which it is applied. The long muscles act at an acute angle, with rapid movement but little power. These short muscles being in direct line produce great power but are relatively slow. The fastest movement of the thumb is therefore slow compared to that of the fingers; its power is proportionately greater.

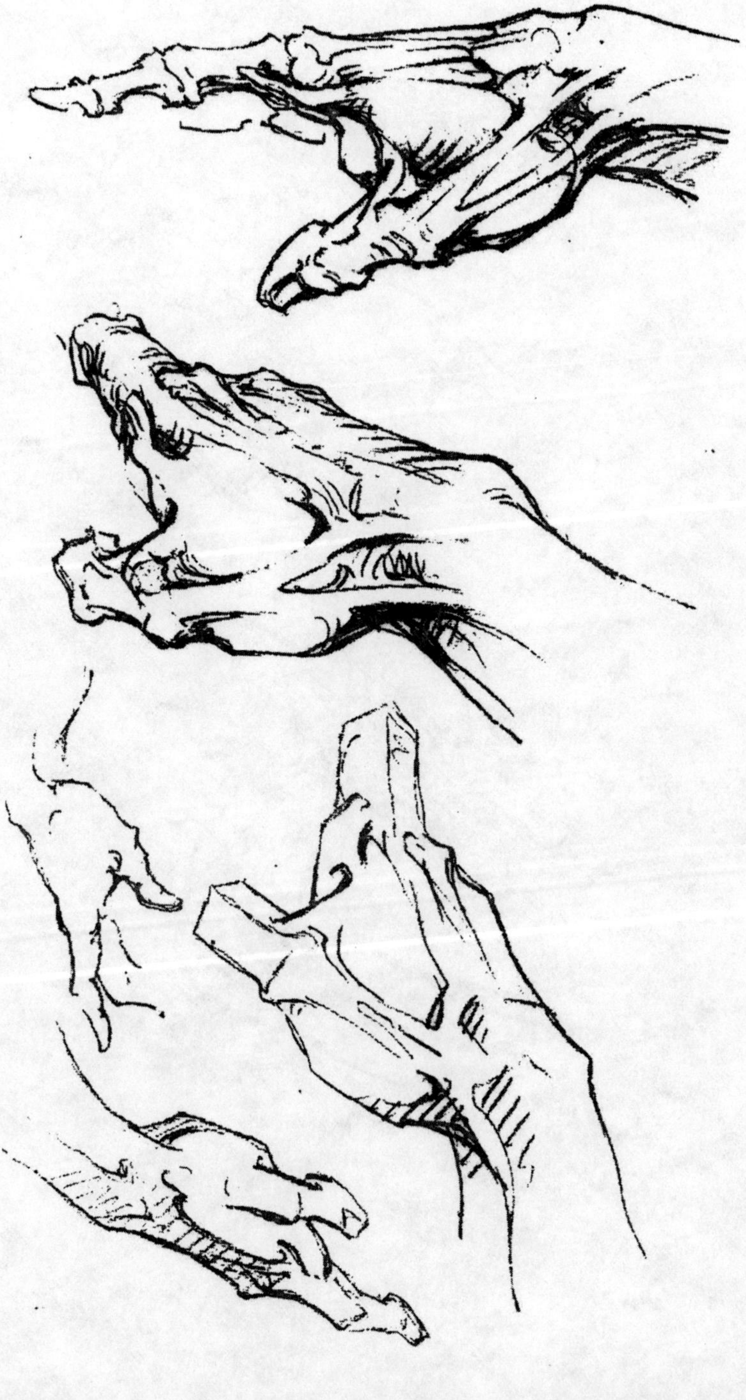

THE HAND
Thumb Side

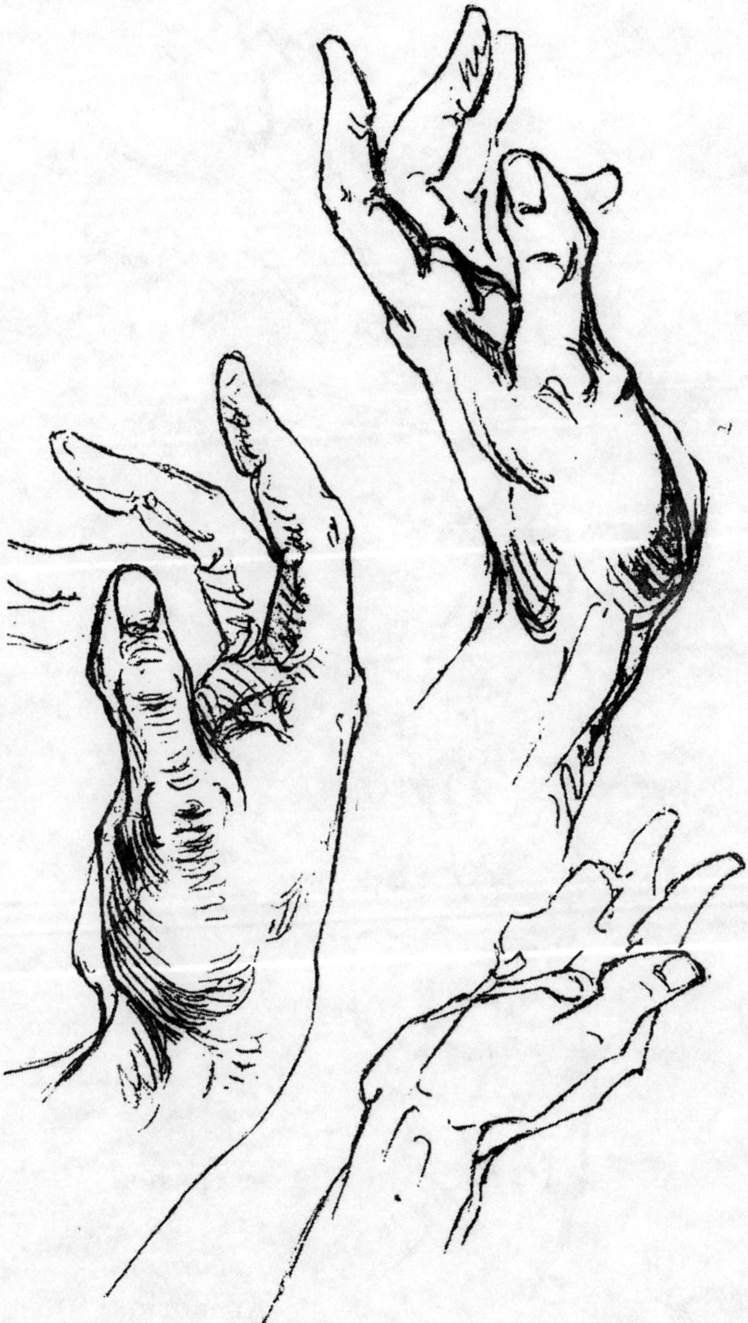

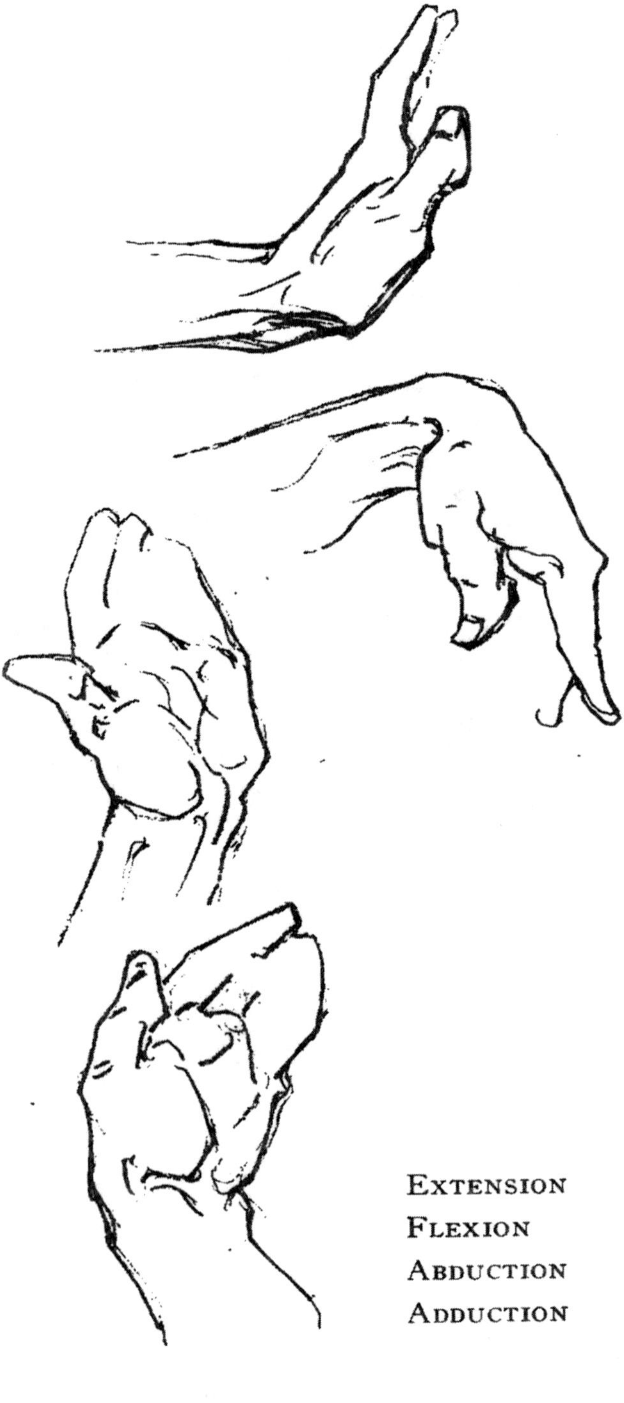

EXTENSION
FLEXION
ABDUCTION
ADDUCTION

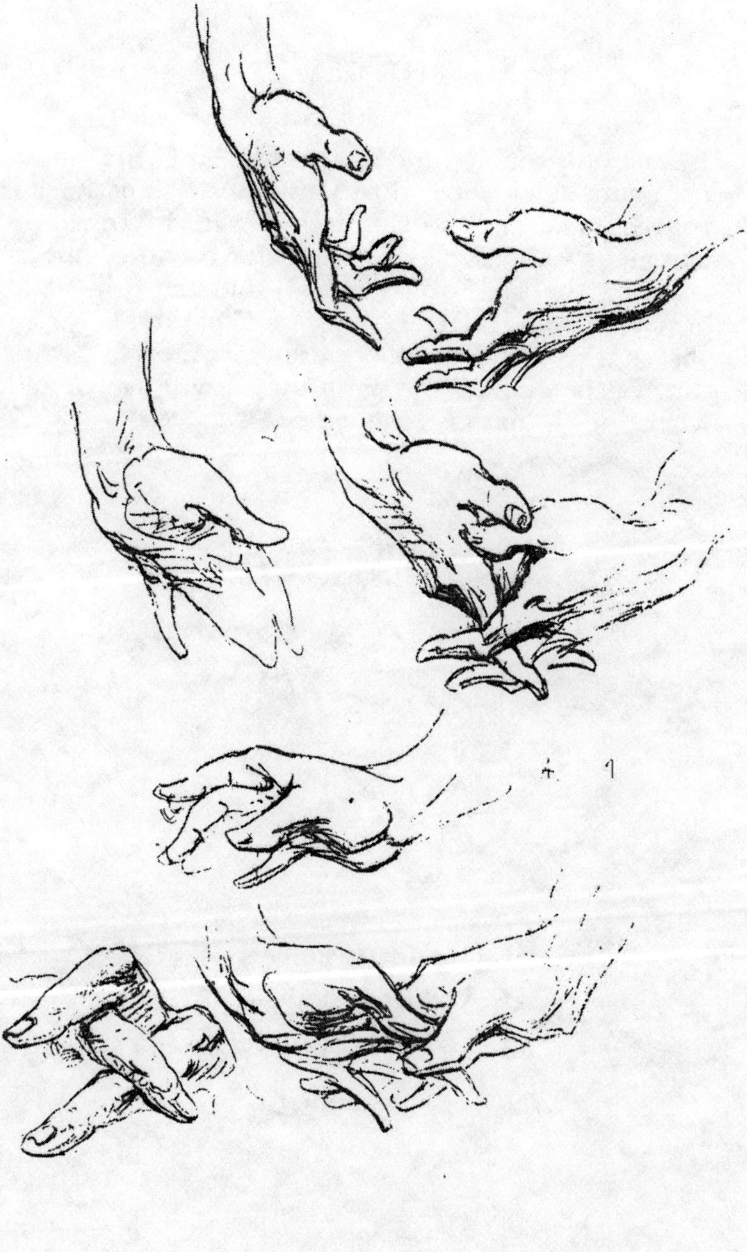

THE HAND

Thumb Side

Distinguishable under the skin of the thumb (palmar side) are three muscles, sometimes a fourth. These, from the back forward, are the fat opponens, hugging the bone; the broad abductor, forming the bulk of the mass; and the thin flexor brevis, inside. Deeper and reaching transversely across the hand is the adductor muscle, which throws the skin of the palm into a bulging wrinkle when the thumb is flattened back.

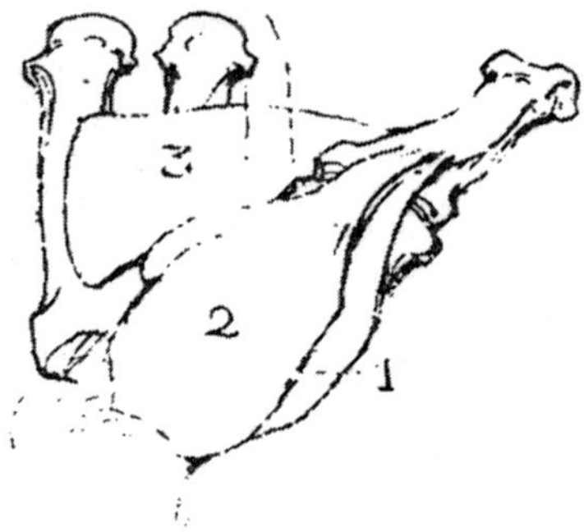

1 Opponens pollicis.

2 Abductor pollicis.

3 Adductor transversus.

Pages 169-171

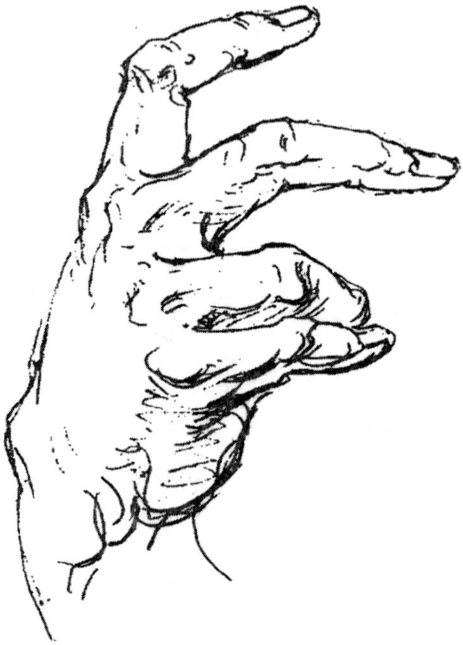

THE HAND

Thumb Side

The little finger side of the hand is the pushing side; the little finger side of the wrist is the heel side. The thumb side of the hand is the pulling side. Since pulling is so much more important a function of the hand, the thumb side of hand and wrist and all the bones of that side, with the first two fingers, are larger.

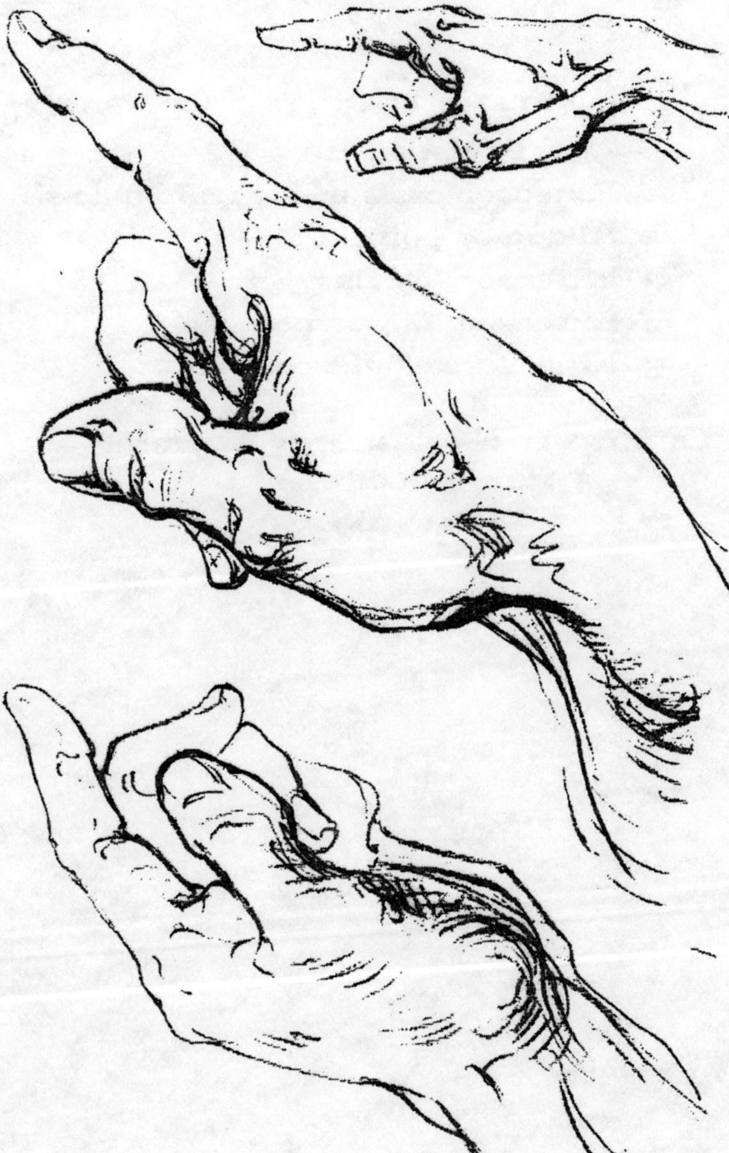

THE HAND

Thumb Side

1 Extensor ossis metacarpi pollicis.

2 Abductor pollicis.

3 Extensor brevis pollicis.

4 Extensor longus pollicis.

5 First dorsal interossei.

Origin, Insertion and Action of Muscles
Page 169

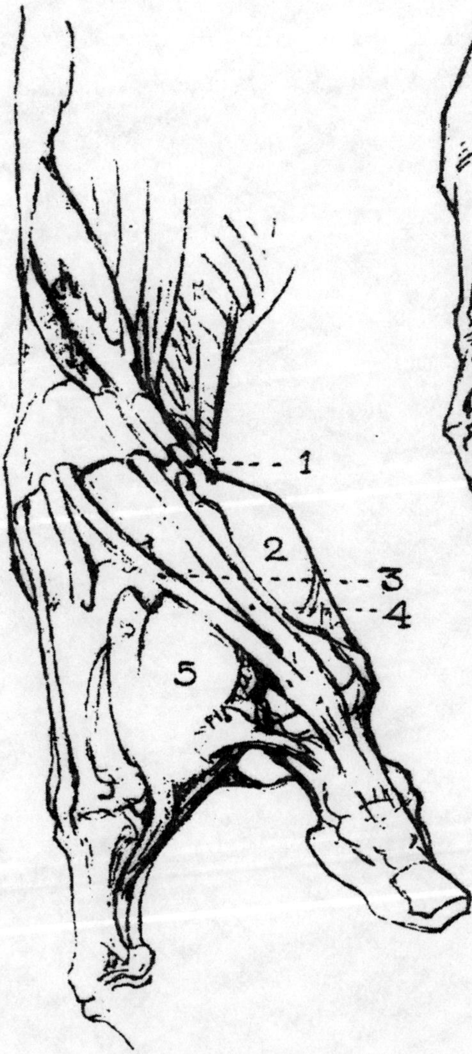
1
2
3
4
5

THE HAND
Little Finger Side

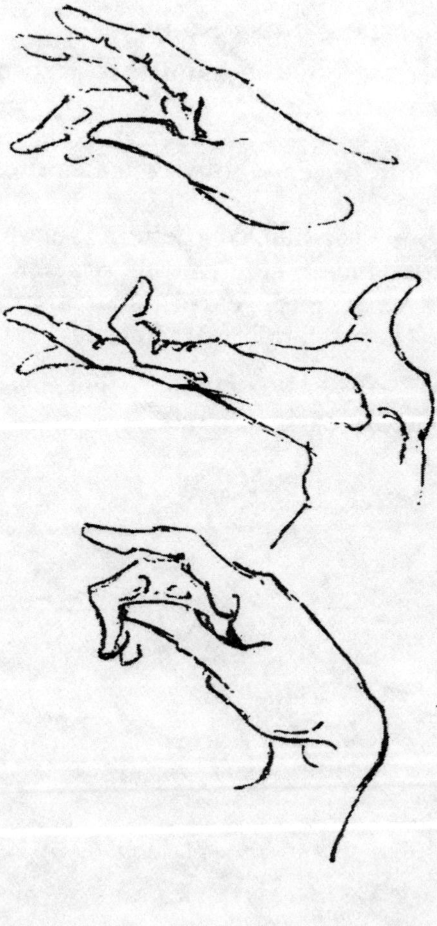

THE HAND

Little Finger Side

The little finger side of the hand sets across the end of the forearm at a sharper angle than does the thumb side.

It is narrower and never wholly conceals the rest of the hand.

The pisiform bone, or heel of the hand, is always conspicuous on the lower side of the wrist.

To it attaches the flexor carpi ulnaris muscle, corresponding with the tendon of Achilles.

1 Pisiform (pea-shaped) bone.

2 Flexor carpi ulnaris.

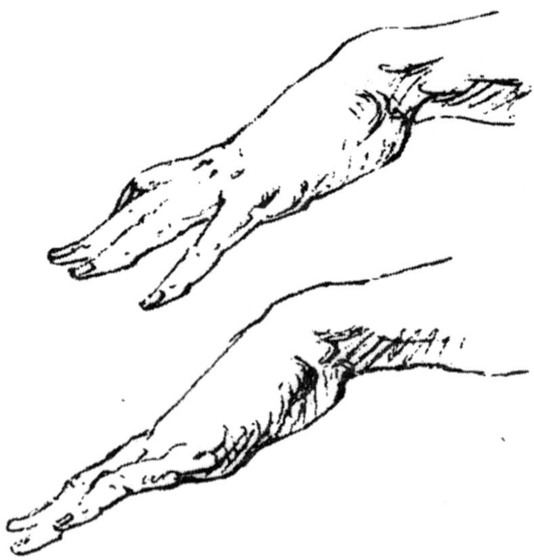

1
2
1
2

THE HAND

Little Finger Side

In resting the wrist on a table, the weight should rest on the pisiform bone. Instinct protects the more sensitive unciform bone, on the thumb end of the wrist arch.

In this position the fingers are always curled up or arched, on account of the shortness of the flexor tendons.

1 Pisiform bone.

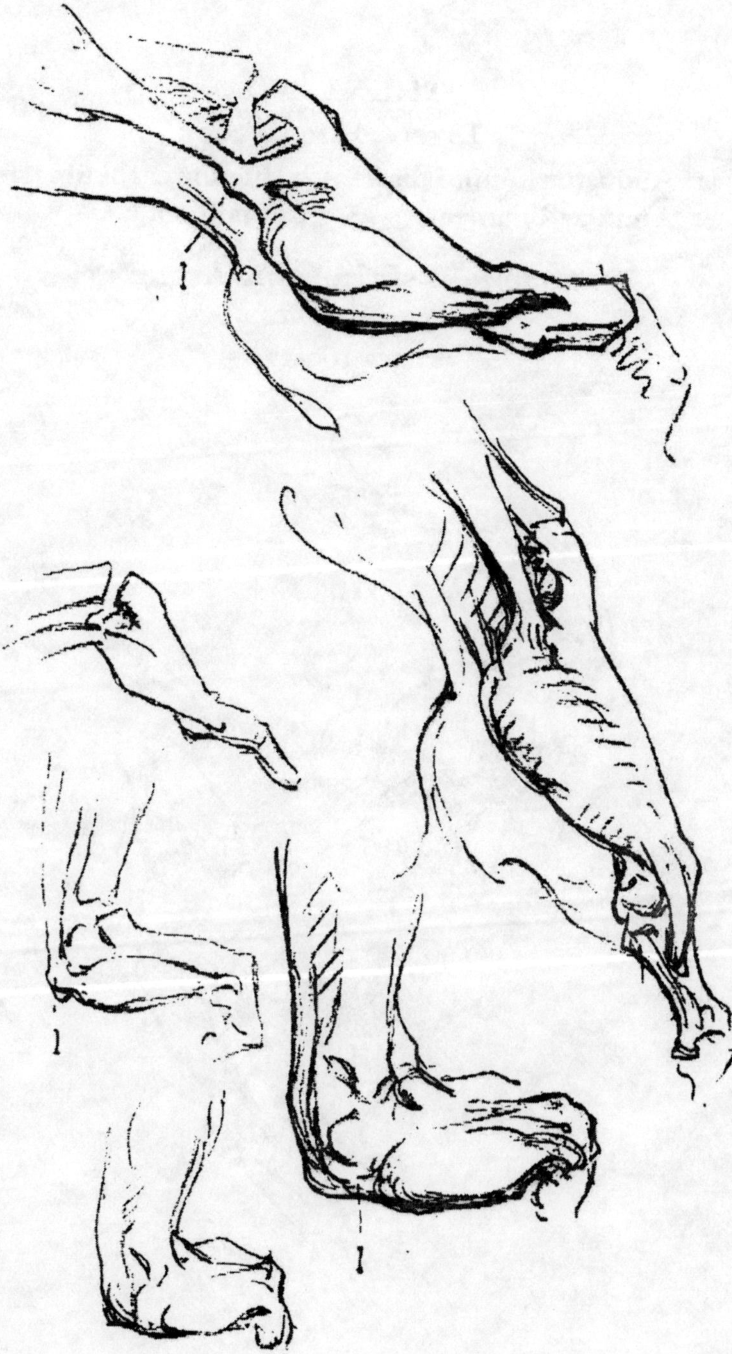

THE HAND

Little Finger Side

1 Abductor minimi digiti.
2 Annular ligament.
3 Flexor carpi ulnaris.
4 Pisiform bone.

Origin, Insertion and Action of Muscles

Pages 169-171

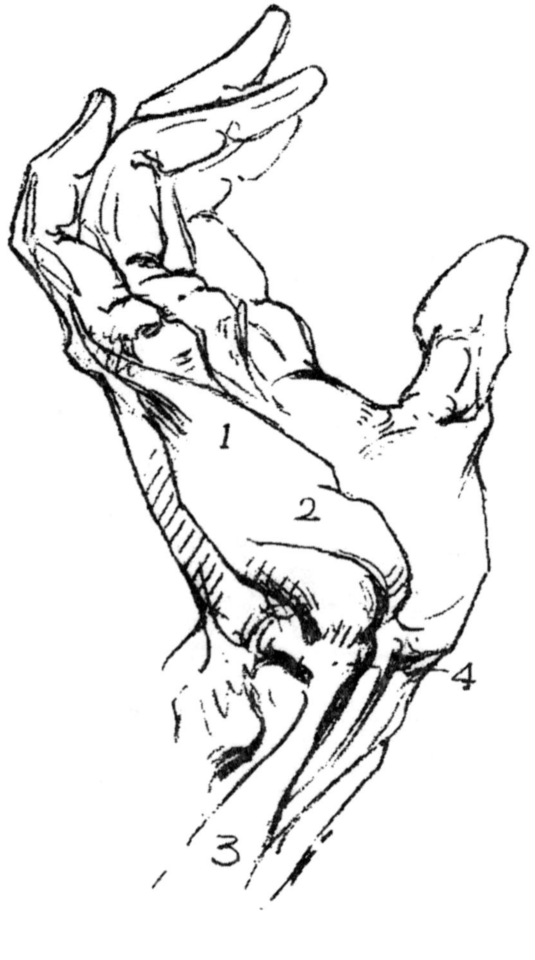

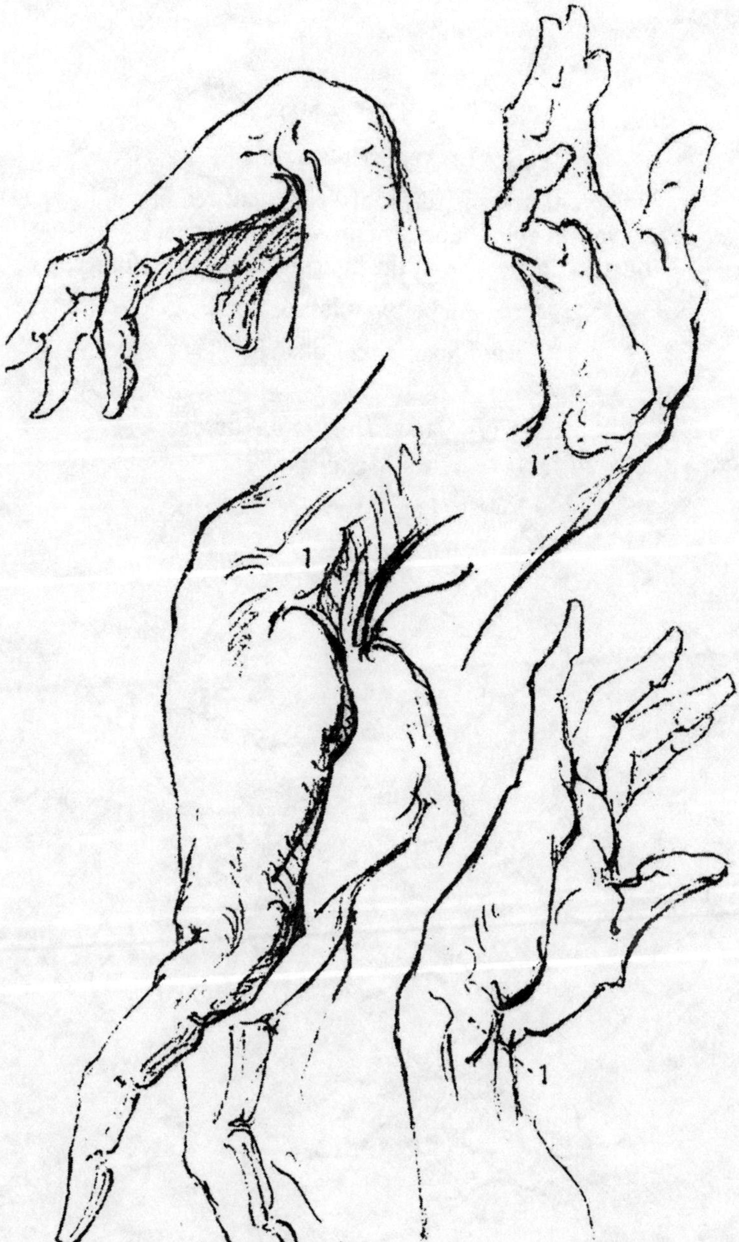
1
1

THE HAND

Little Finger Side

Beyond the pisiform, after a small tendinous interval, is the abductor minimi digiti muscle, running to the outside of the knuckle of the little finger.

1 Abductor minimi digiti.

2 Flexor carpi ulnaris.

Origin, Insertion and Action of Muscles
Pages 169-171

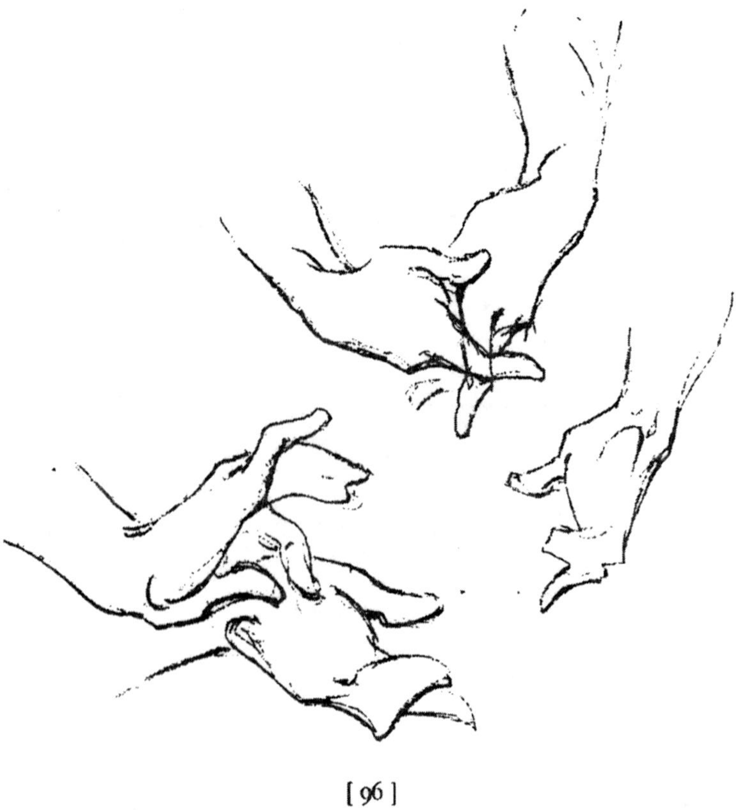

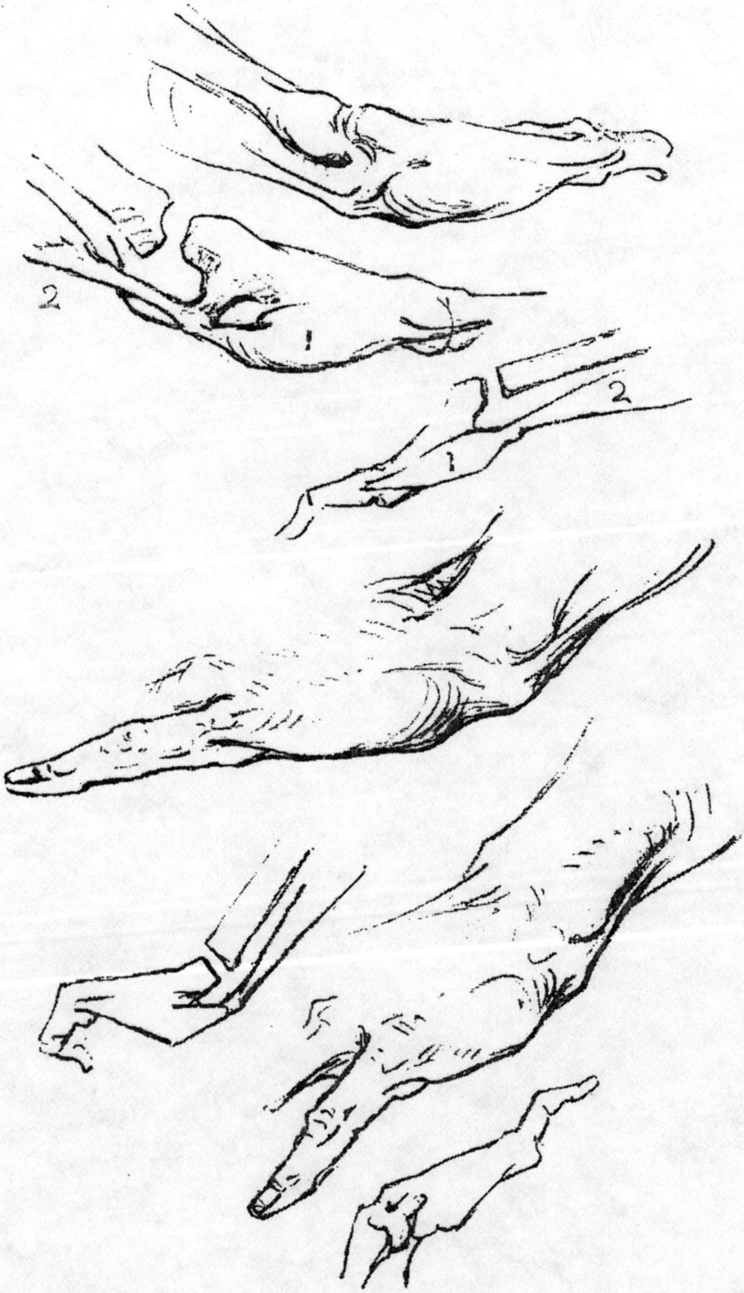
2
1
2
1

THE THUMB

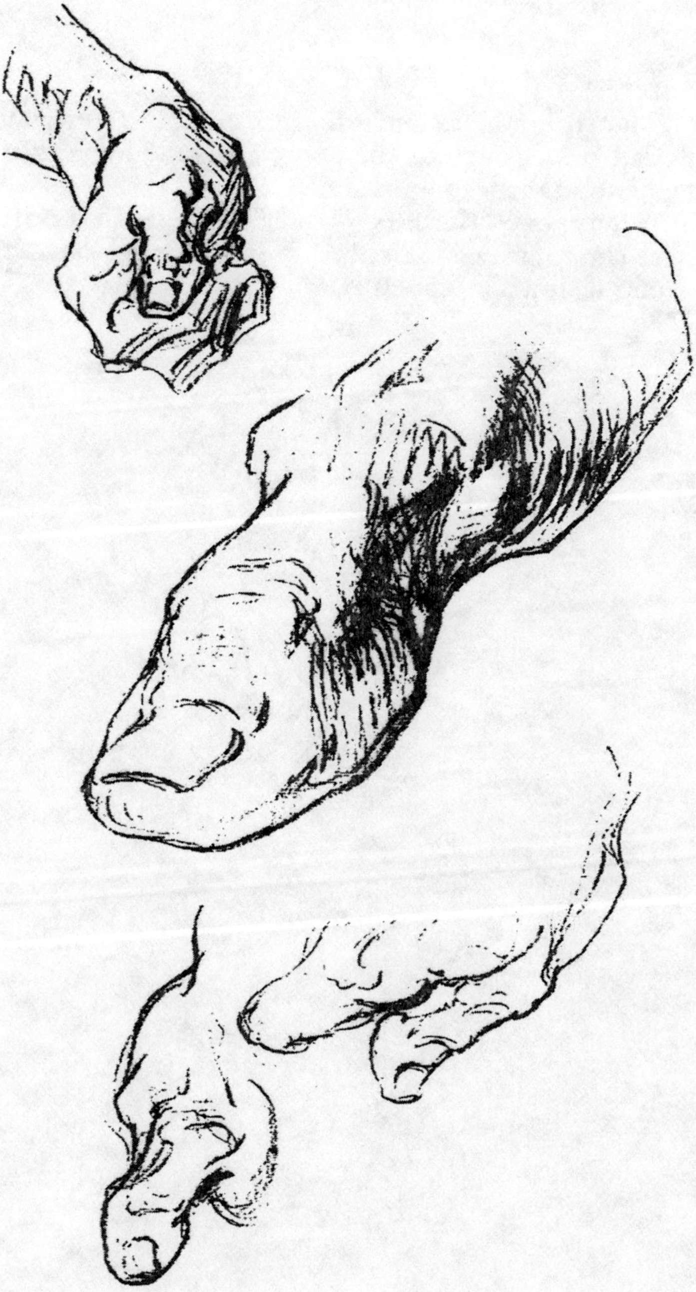

THE THUMB

The thumb, extended, faces half frontways; flexed it faces across the palm, and may by pressure be bent slightly toward it.

It may touch the side of the first finger, but otherwise cannot touch the palm. It is the fingers that are brought down to touch it.

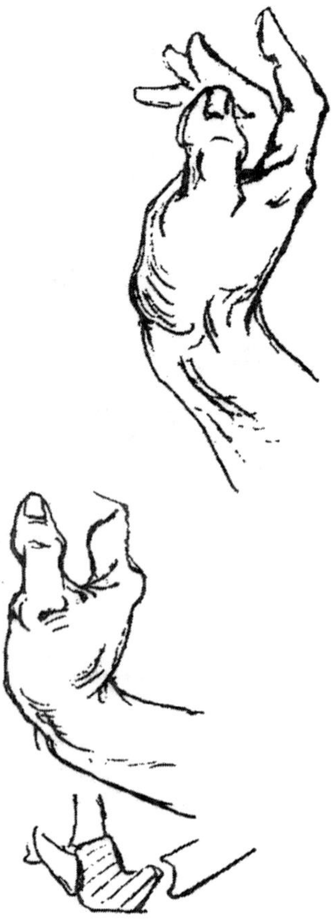

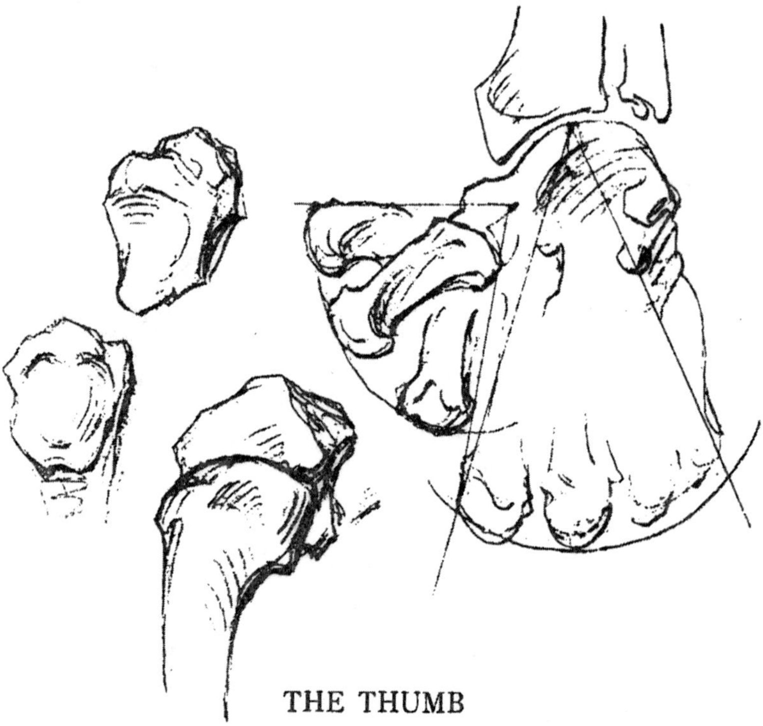

THE THUMB

Saddle Joint

The range of movement of the thumb is slight—half a right angle at the base, much less at the middle joint, a right angle at the last joint.

The basal joint is a saddle joint, permitting half a right angle of movement sideways, and very much less fore and aft. The middle joint is extra large in proportion to others on account of its exposed position, permitting slight flexion and very slight torsion. It is built for strength rather than movement. The last joint with its long muscle reaching to the elbow has a right angle of movement (this long muscle must take up the slack of the other joints, including the wrist, also).

THE THUMB

The mass of the thumb is in three parts. That of the base is pyramidal, extending forward from the radial edge and half of the front side of the hand; its base reaching to the "line of life" of the palm and to the amulet wrinkle of the wrist; its apex at the middle joint. Its faces are rounded and bulging except at the back where the bone is superficial and the thick tendon may be seen.

Angling inward from this apex rises the second part, slender, square with rounded edges, with a thin pad in front.

Balanced sharply backward across this is the last part, pear-shaped, carrying the nail. Its skin pad, or ball, faces to the front more than sideways. It is broad at the base, where it covers the exposed extremity of the middle segment in extension, giving an appearance not unlike a foot as it presses against some object. Its tip reaches to the middle joint of the first finger.

The mass of the thumb may bend under the hand to about the centre, where it is invisible from the back except a curved root. It may bend out to about a right angle. It bends back very slightly if at all, except at the tip. Between thumb and palm, as also on the back, a roll of flesh may be raised by pressure of the thumb, and is drawn into a thin curved blade when stretched.

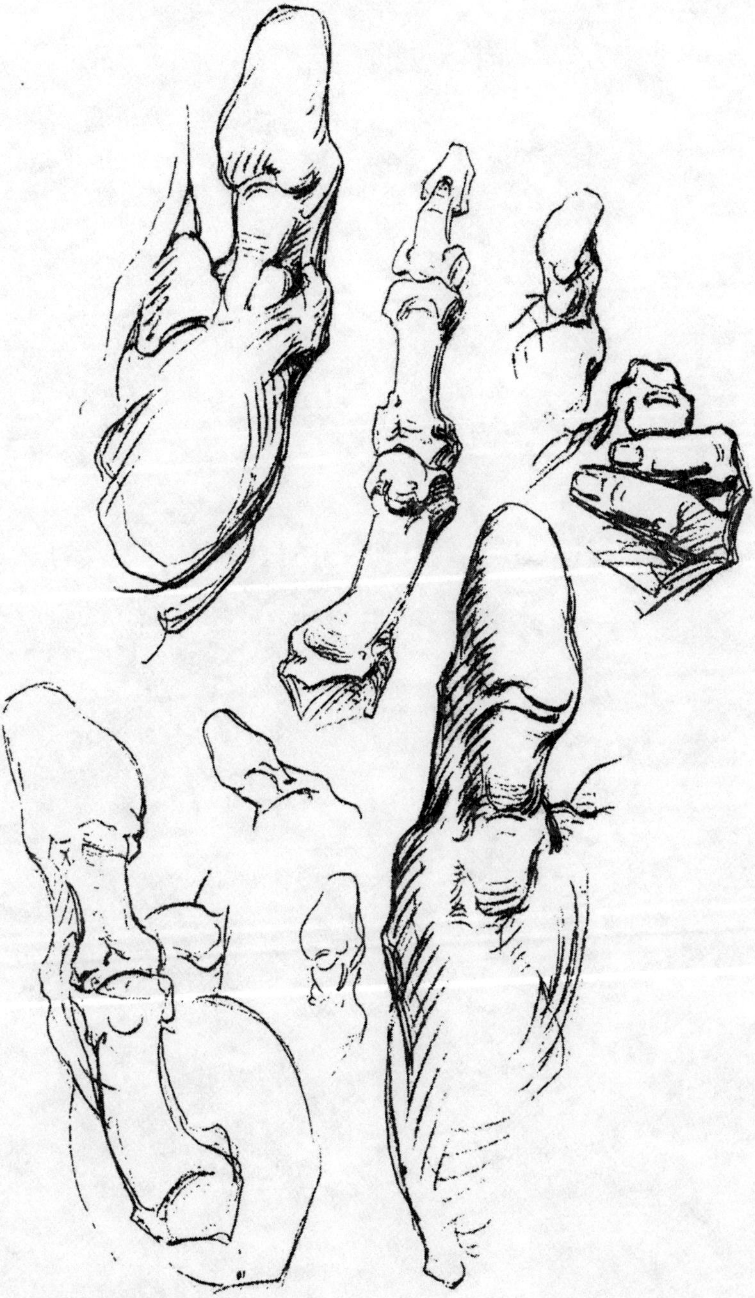

THE THUMB

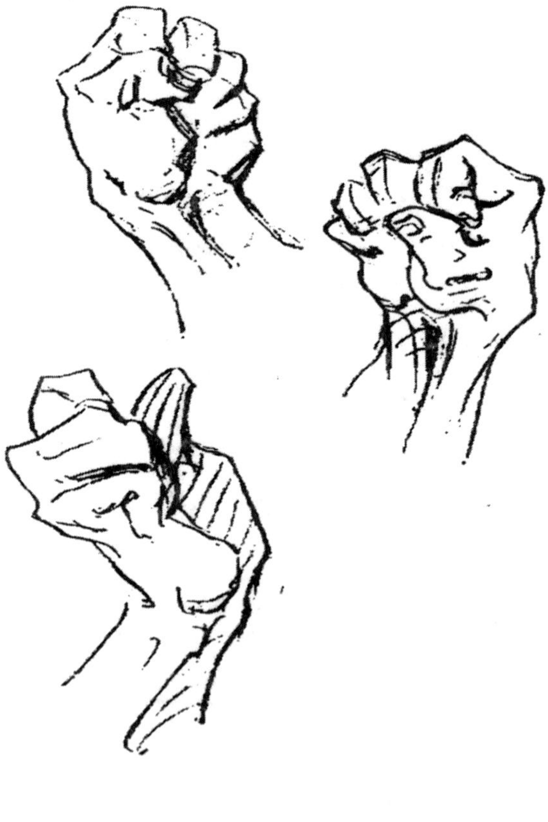

FINGERS

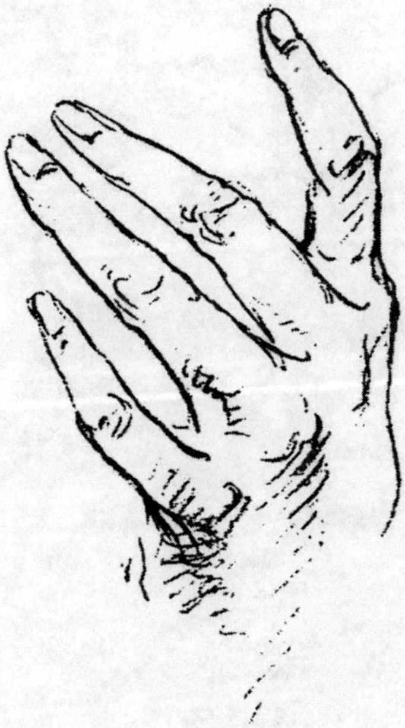

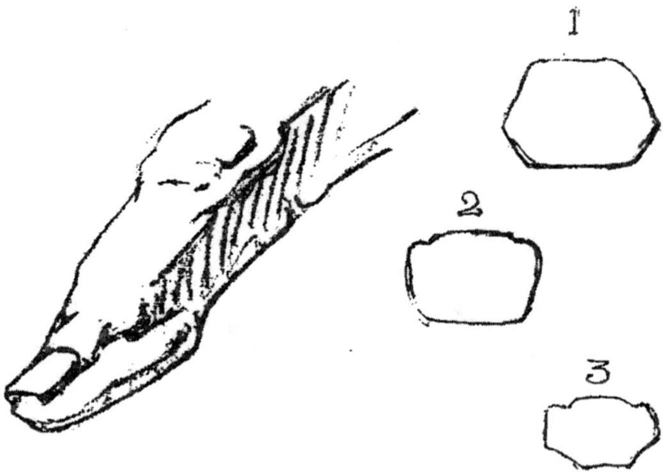

FINGERS

1 SECTIONAL VIEW—First finger between knuckle and second joint.

2 SECTIONAL VIEW—Between second and third joint.

3 SECTIONAL VIEW—Last joint at nail.

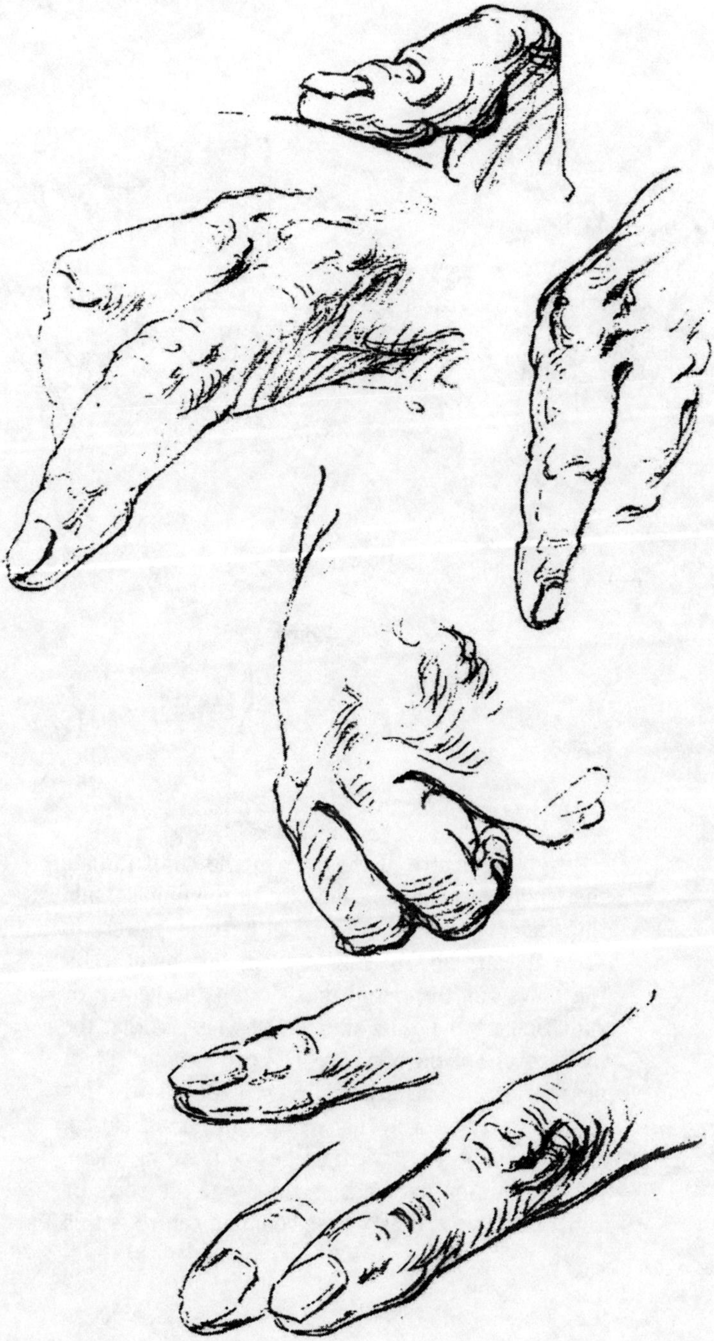

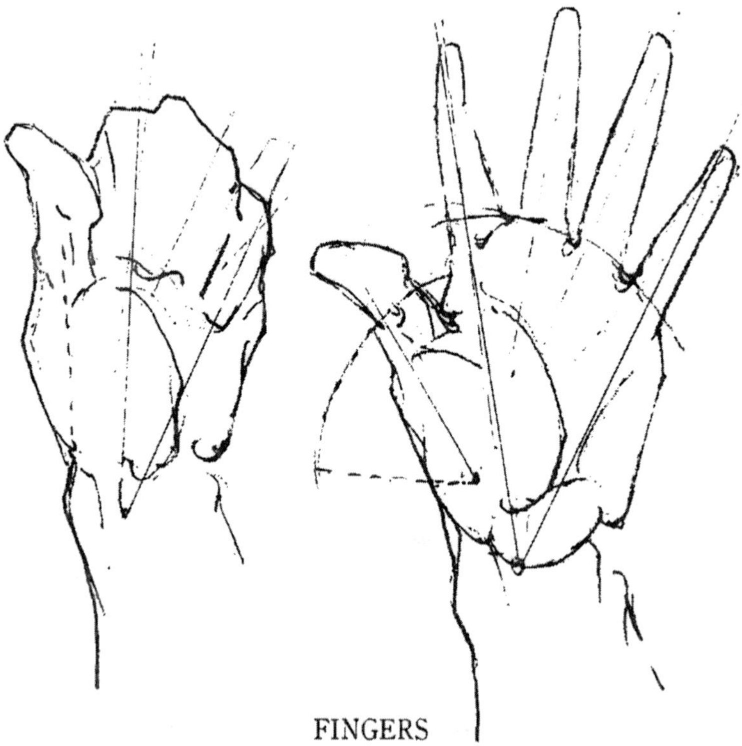

FINGERS

From the centre of the arch of the wrist radiate the tendons of the long muscles to the fingers; and the fingers must be in line with their power, to prevent warping, so radiate from this point. But the power of the thumb has drawn the centre of radiation a trifle to its side of the wrist, so that the mechanisms of the hand are grouped around a point near its base. The clenched fingers all point to this centre, as far as crowding will permit. Half closed, as in clasping, they form arches converging there. In any position except a strained one the rows of knuckles form arches whose common centre is this point.

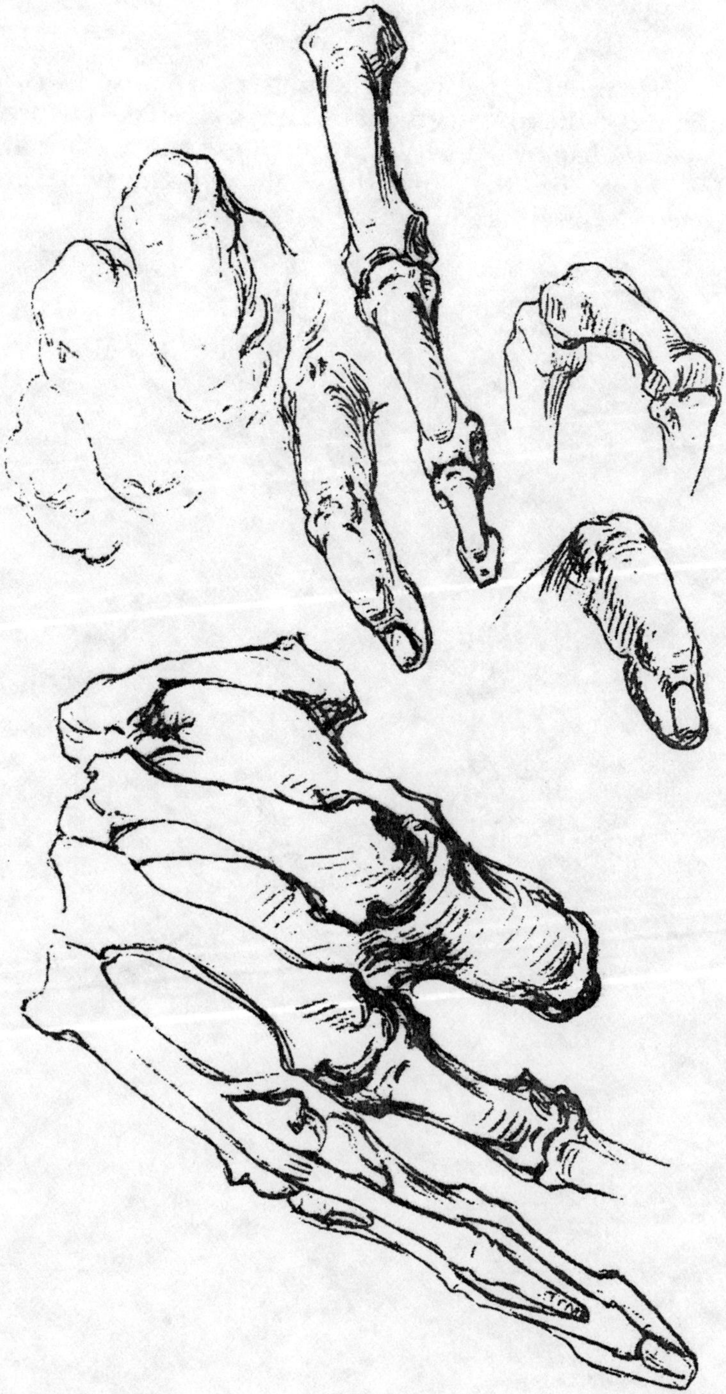

FINGERS

The webbing between the fingers runs up to the middle of the first segment on the palm side. Thence it bevels backward between the fingers to a point at the apex of the knuckles; which point it never reaches, but sinks in between the knuckles.

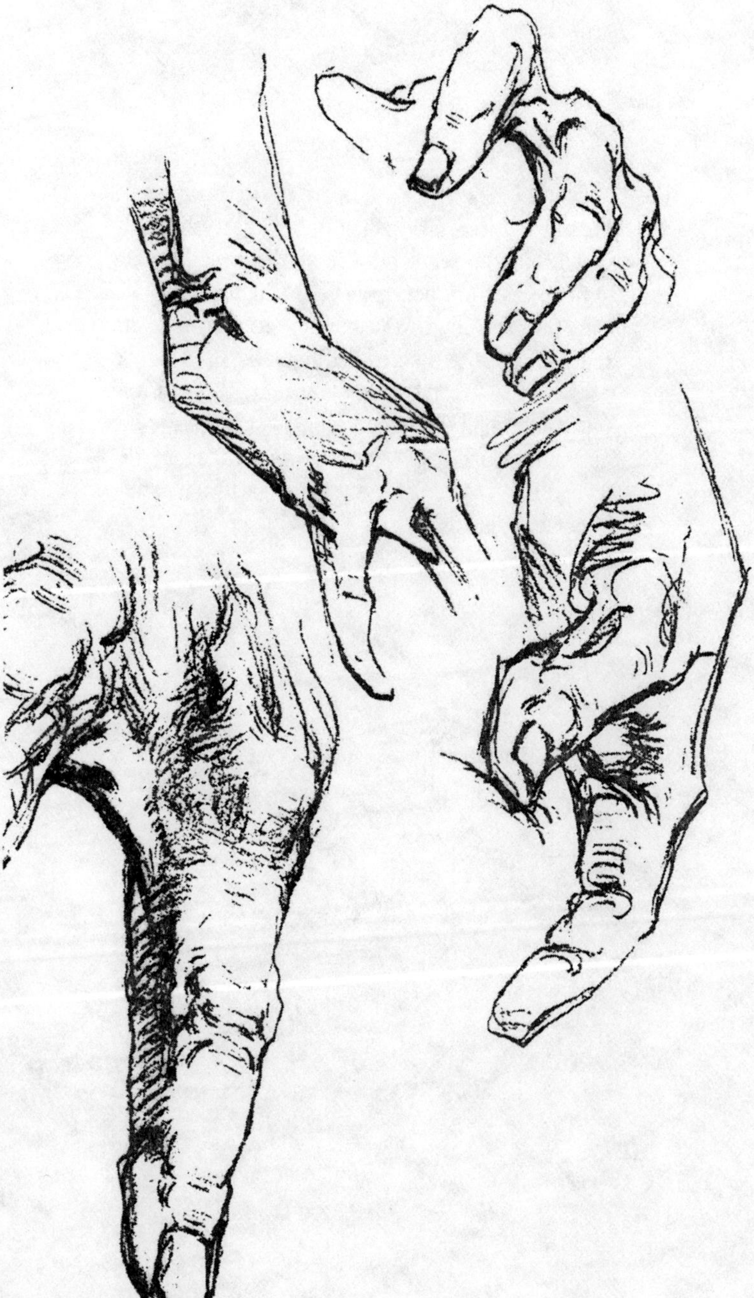

FINGERS

The skin pads are of approximately the same length, as necessary when the finger is tightly closed, but the segments are of different lengths; so the creases are not opposite the joints.

In the first finger the creases are beyond the knuckle, opposite the middle joint, and short of the last; in the second finger they are beyond the knuckle, beyond the second joint, about opposite the last; in the third finger they are beyond the knuckle, beyond the second. The other positions vary in different individuals.

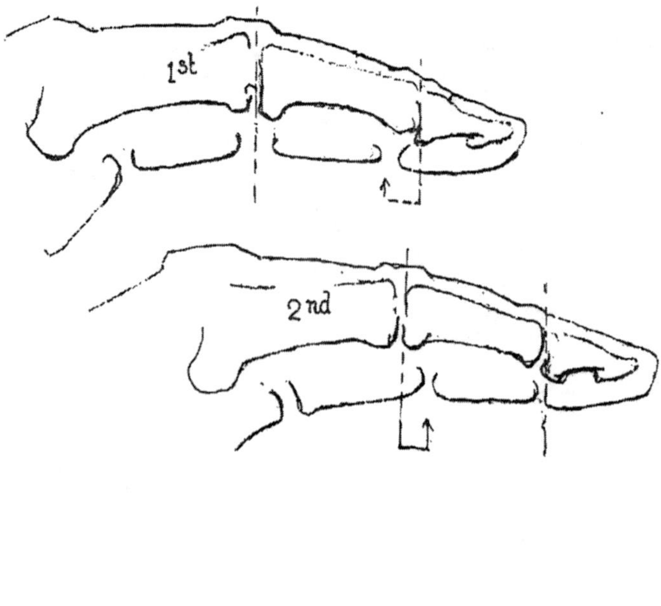

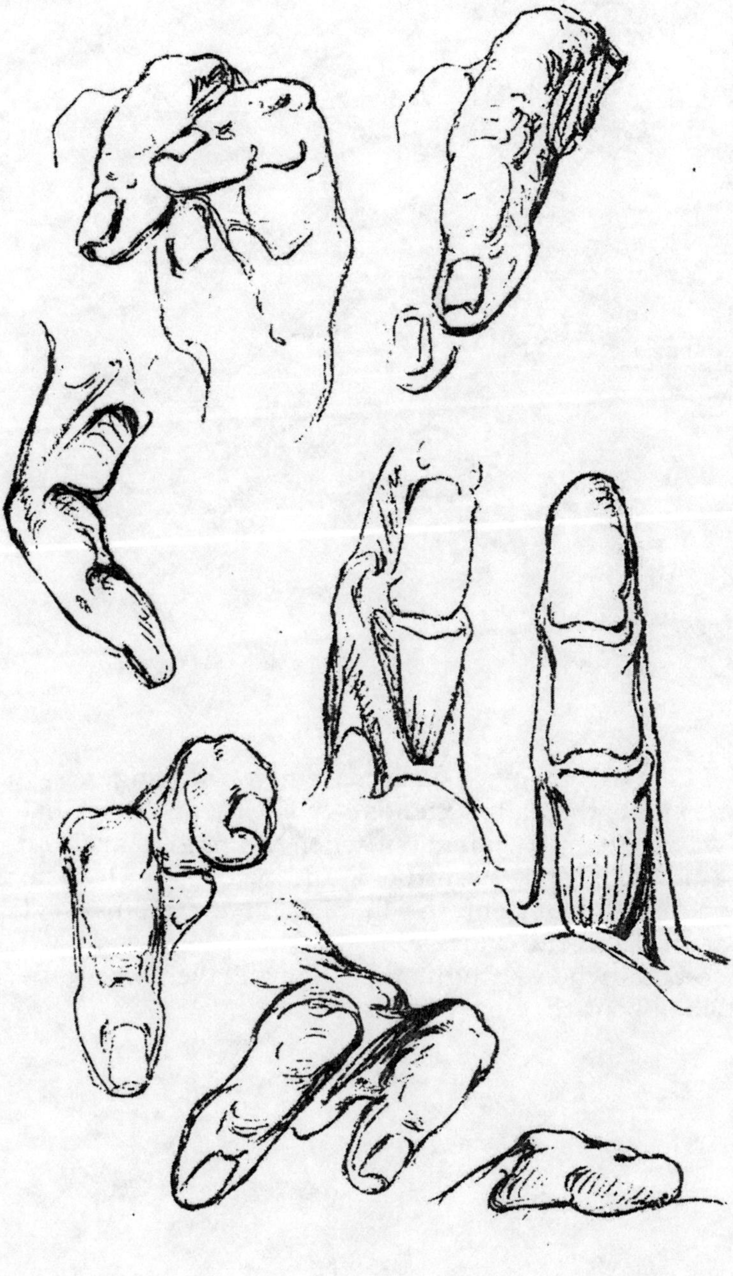

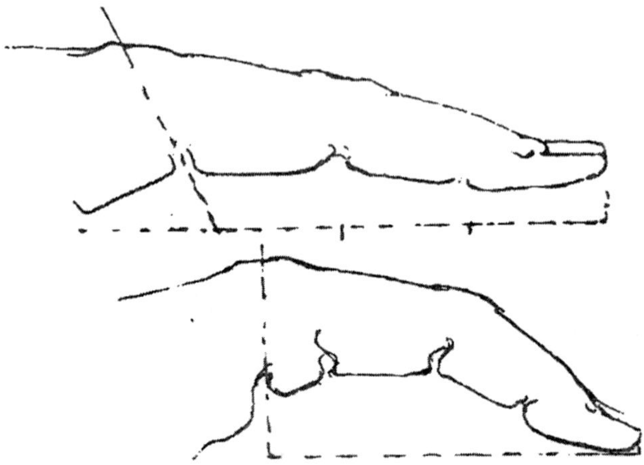

FINGERS

On the palmar surface, when the fingers are straight, the palm extends beyond the knuckles half way to the next joint; but when the fingers are bent, a portion bends with them, and belongs with them; so that when bent the fingers on the palmar side start from the knuckle.

Thus when straight the fingers have three pads; when bent they have four.

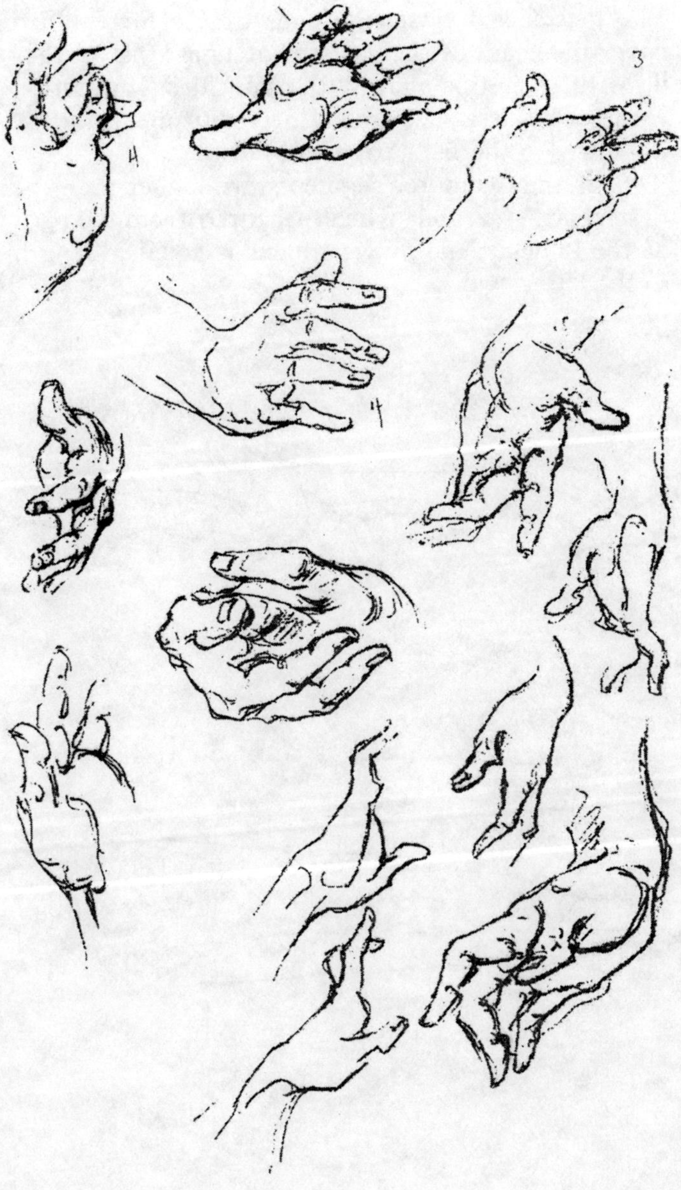

FINGERS

When curled close, the ends of the fingers just cover the heads of their first phalanges; that is, they lie with their tips against the knuckles, supporting them. This is a mechanical necessity in fitting the fingers into the fist (page 124).

Thus the two outer segments are longer than the first (page 130), but when measured from the back of the knuckle, the first segment is equal in length to the latter two.

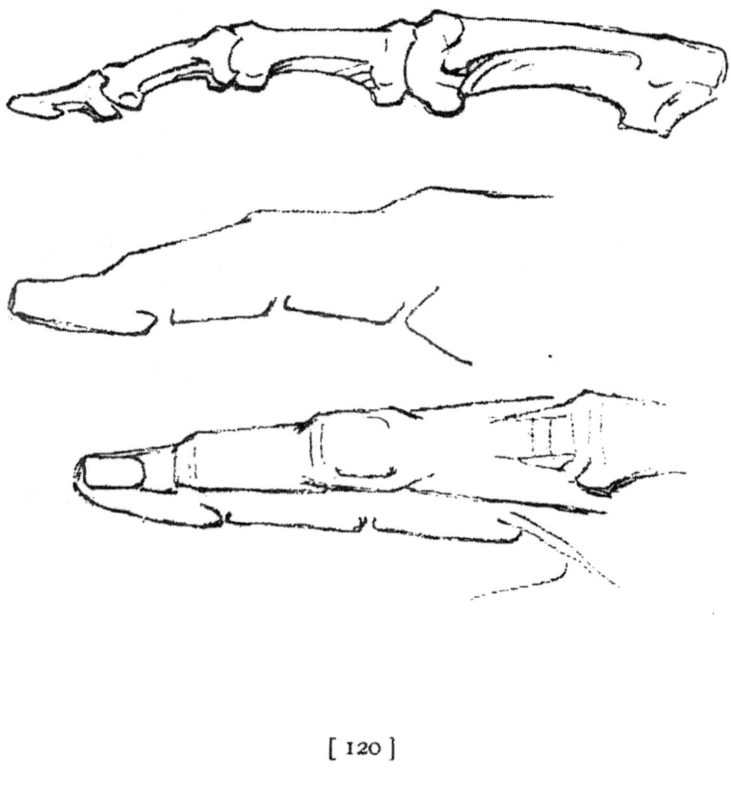

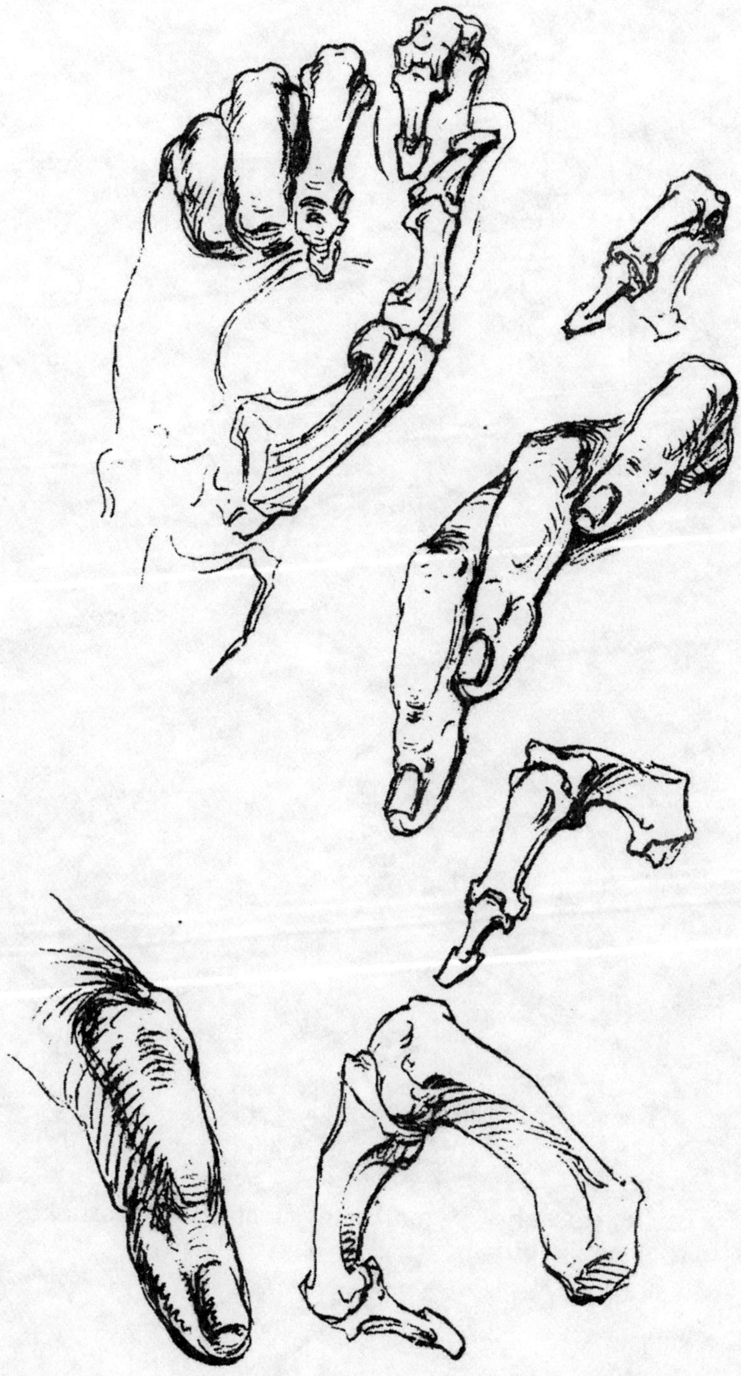

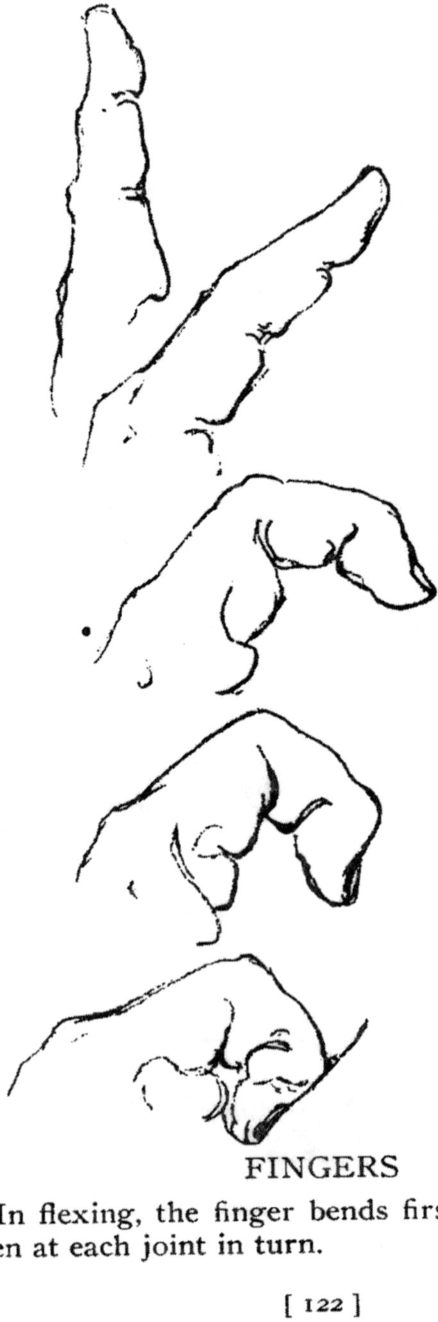

FINGERS

In flexing, the finger bends first at the knuckle, then at each joint in turn.

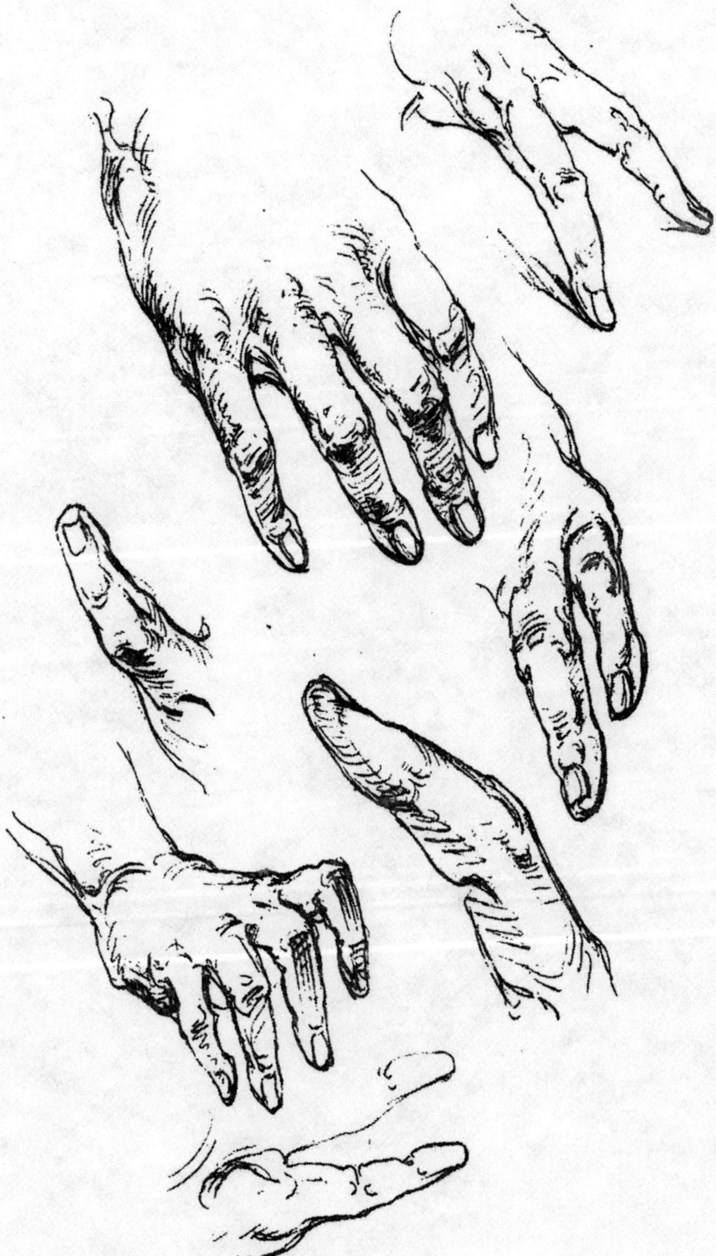

FINGERS

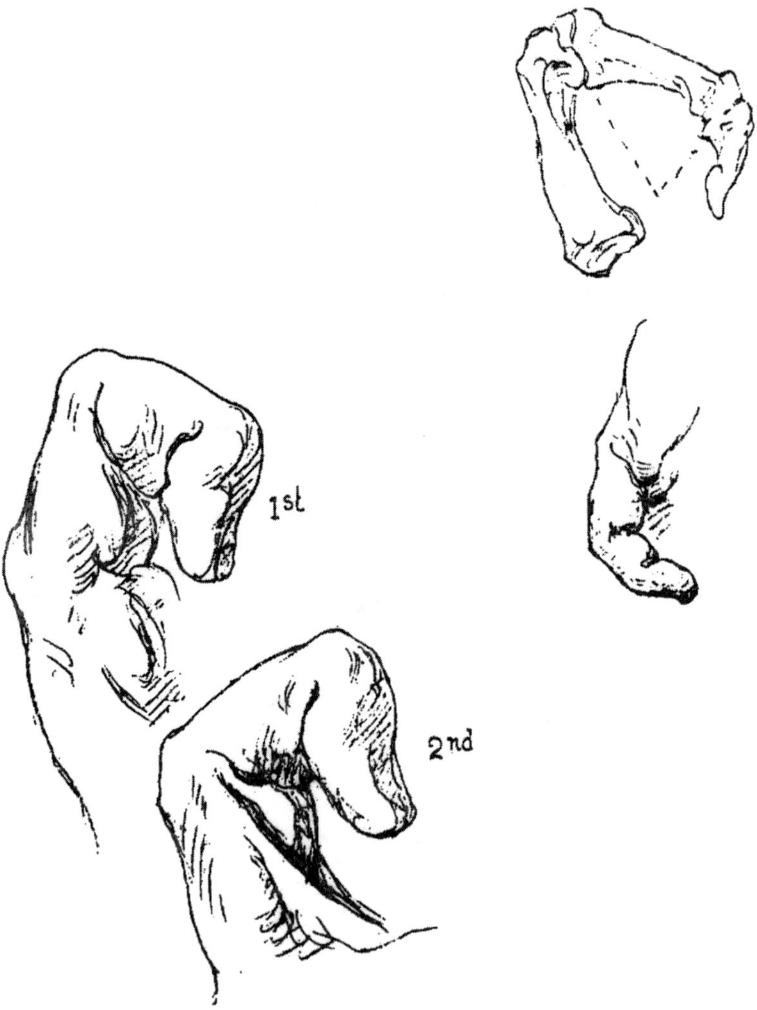

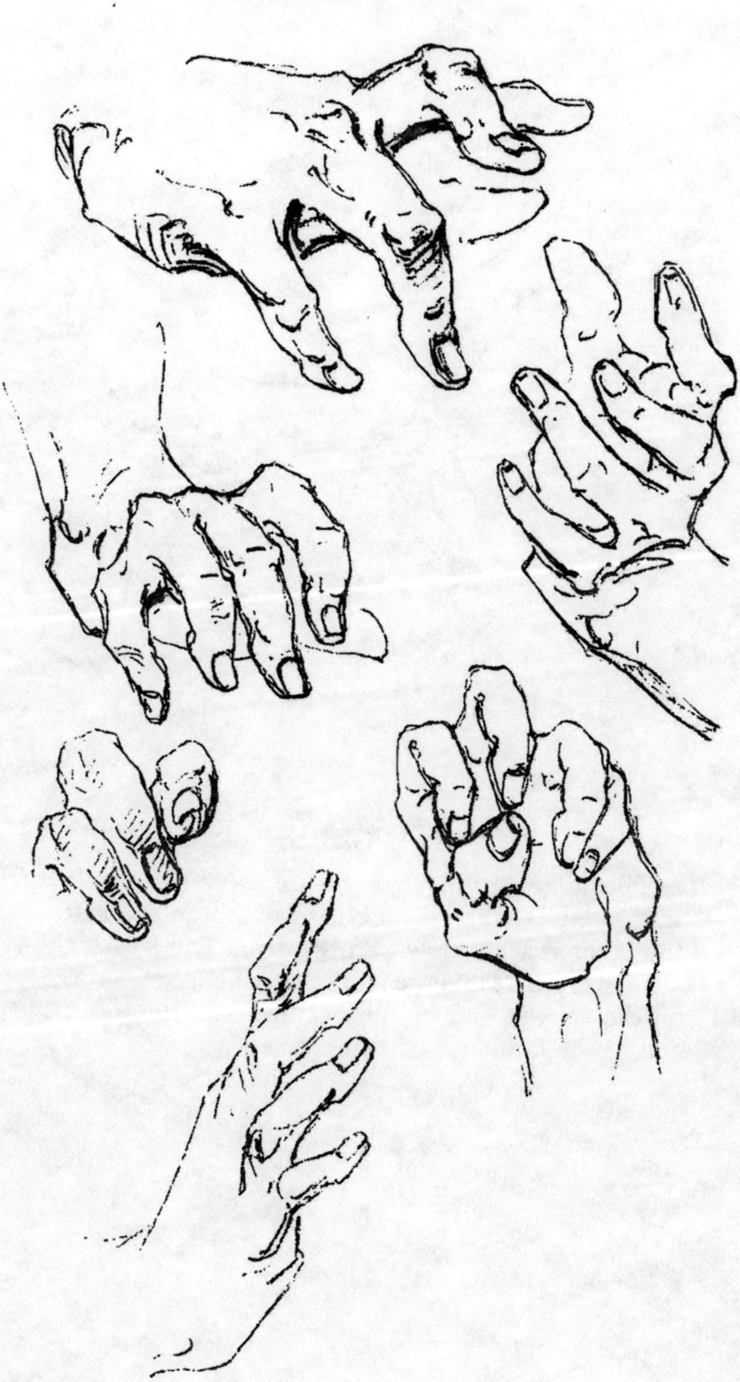

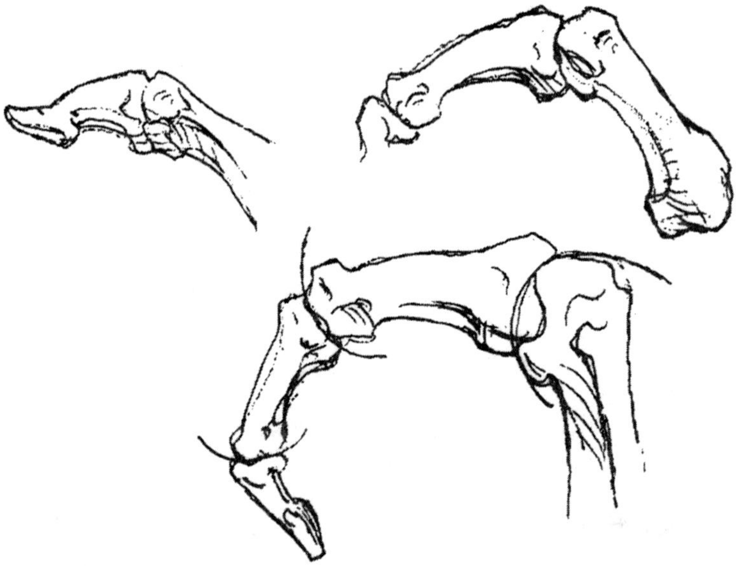

FINGERS

The joints of the fingers are built like shallow saddle joints; that is, one reaches up on the sides, the other reaches down on the front and back.

In every case it is the more distant bone that turns on the convex end of the nearer bone, leaving the end of the latter exposed in flexion.

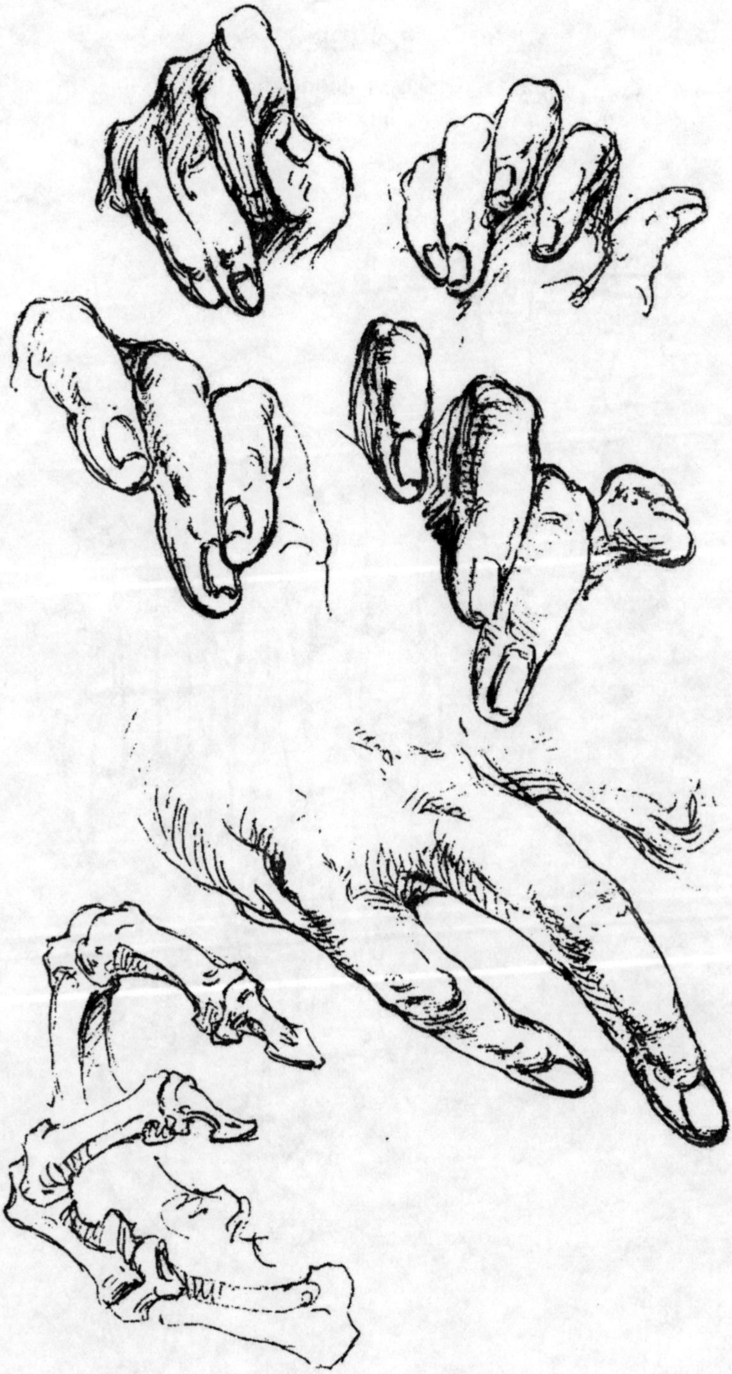

FINGERS

1, 2, 3, 4 Bones, tendons and sheathing of the fingers, palm side.

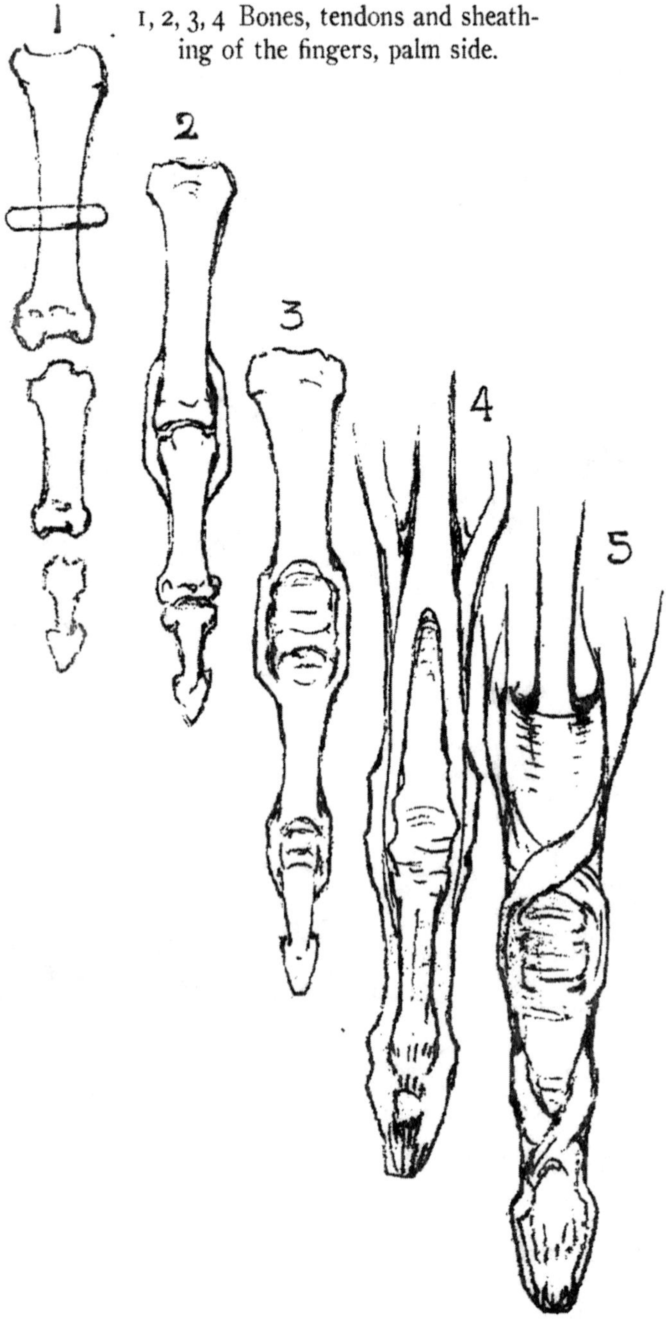

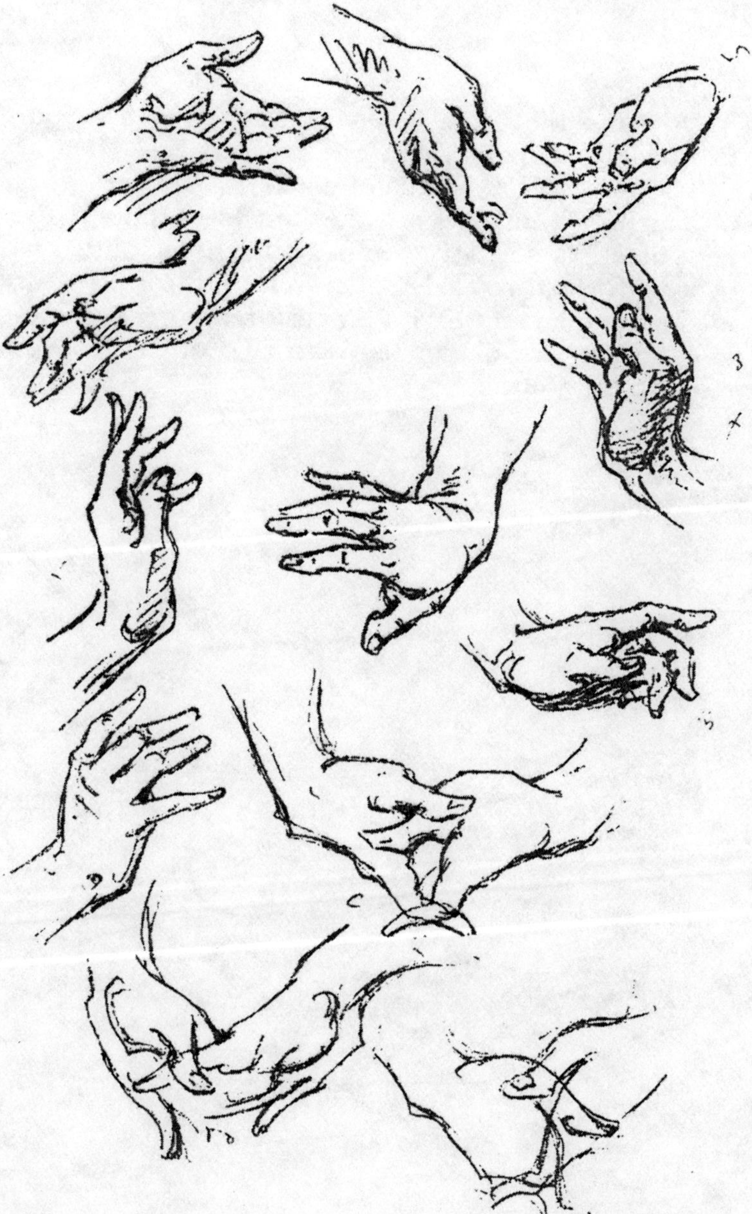

FINGERS

Opposite the three bones of the finger are four skin pads; the pads therefore smaller.

The first joint is about equal to the last two, measuring from back of the knuckle (though the bone itself is shorter). When the three joints are bent to form three sides of a square, the four pads fill in the quarters of it. Three of the grooves between them are diagonals, with two other grooves irregularly placed.

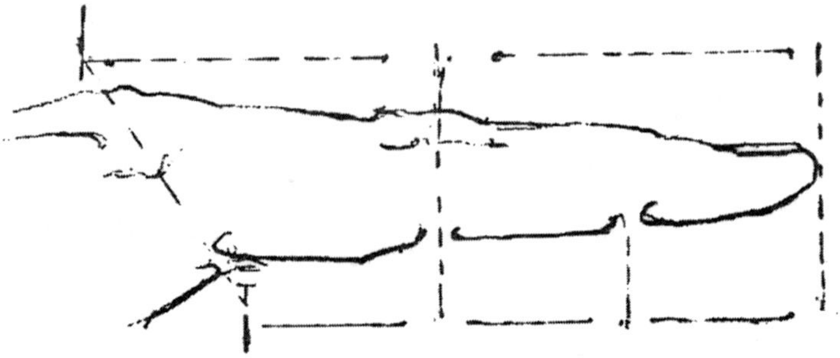

KNUCKLES

There is no muscular covering for the knuckles; only the tendons, which are half blended with them, and roughened skin.

In clenching, this skin is tightly stretched, and by contact with objects is hardened, so that in other positions it is wrinkled.

The end of the metacarpal bone is a round dome, over which fits the socket of the first phalanx. The dome is protected on the sides by square projecting flanges, which are matched by the sides of the socket. They are in the first finger set at a slight diagonal, so that there is an overhang of the phalanx, serving to protect the joint in lateral blows.

KNUCKLES

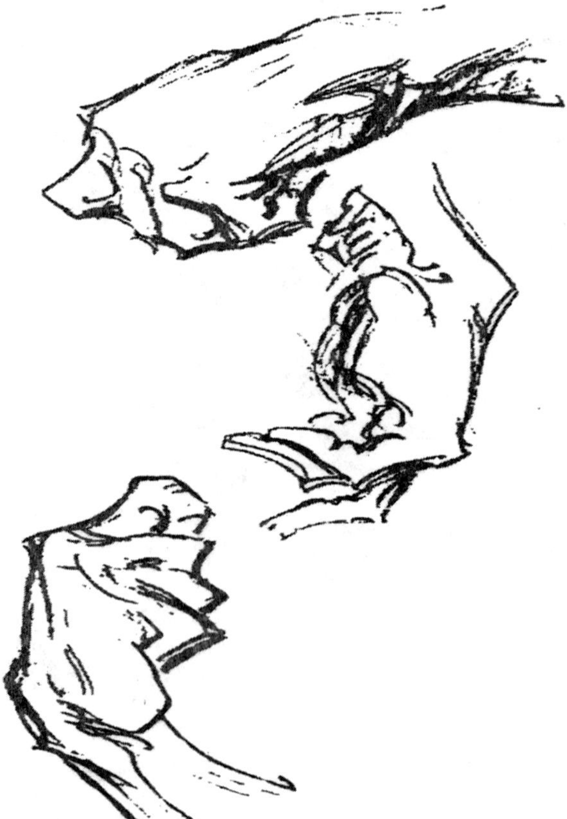

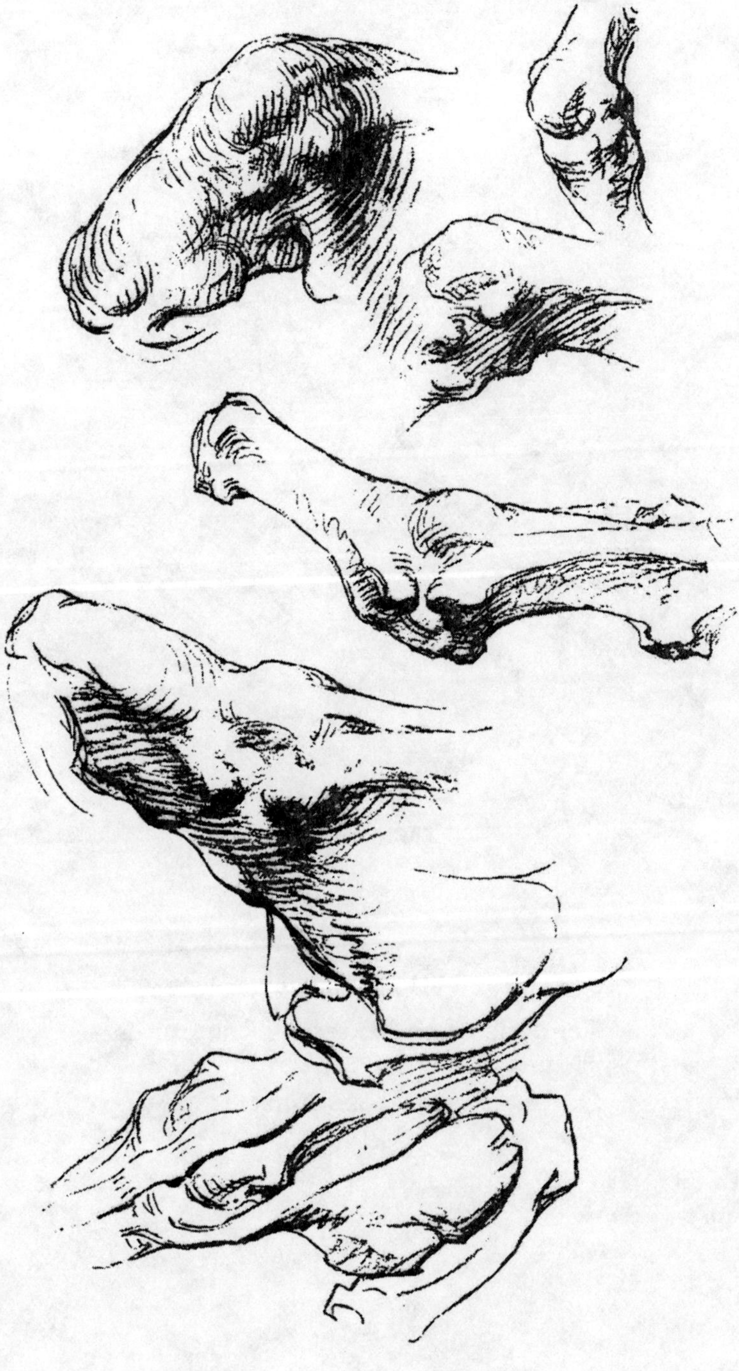

KNUCKLES

1 Tendons of the extensor communis digitorum.

2 Dorsal interosseous muscles.

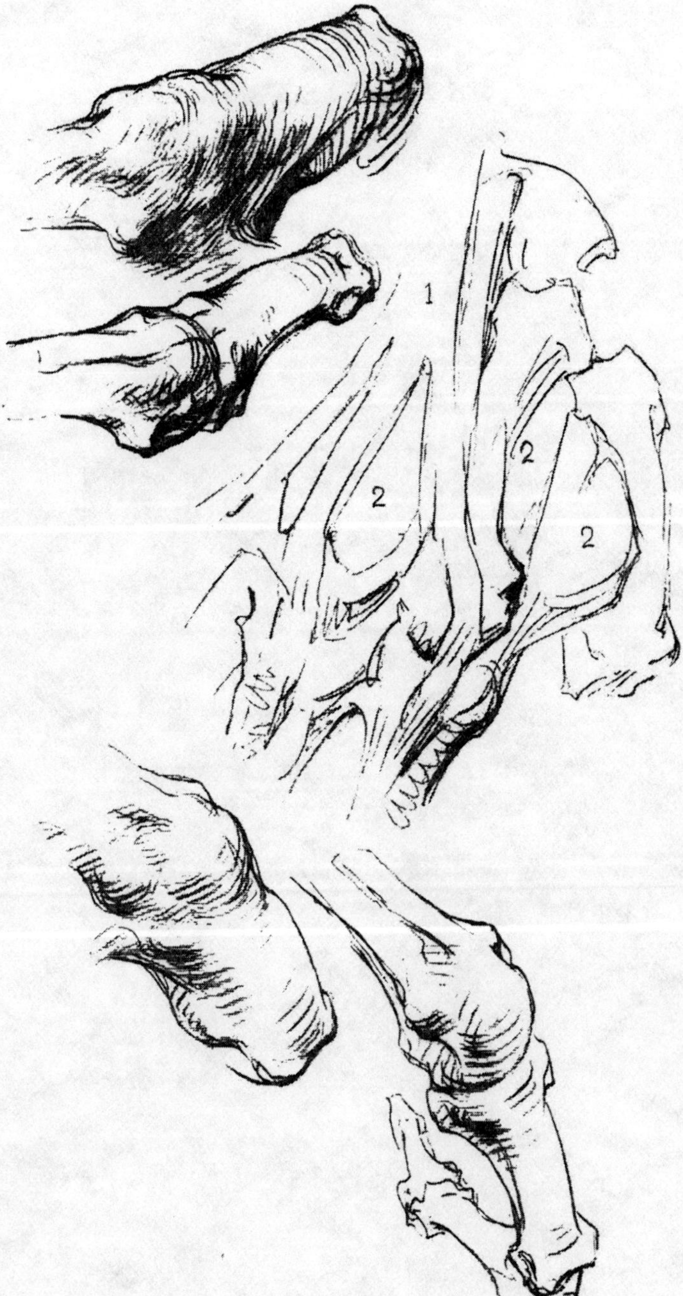
1
2
2
2

THE FIST

THE FIST

The hand, open, is an implement.

The hand, closed, is a weapon.

When driven forward, the second knuckle, as the most prominent, becomes the point of impact; but in clenching it is braced by the entire fist, bone, tendon and knuckle.

When driven directly forward, the second knuckle is in line with the wrist and the radius, making a straight battering ram.

THE FIST

The fist bends back to almost a right angle with the forearm, and bends forward to slightly less; but between front edge and back edge of the fist is a considerable angle; so that its total movement in this direction is barely more than one right angle. The amount of lateral bending is barely more than half a right angle.

The fist bends more easily backward than forward, and more easily to the little finger side than to the thumb side, on account of the position in clasping an object.

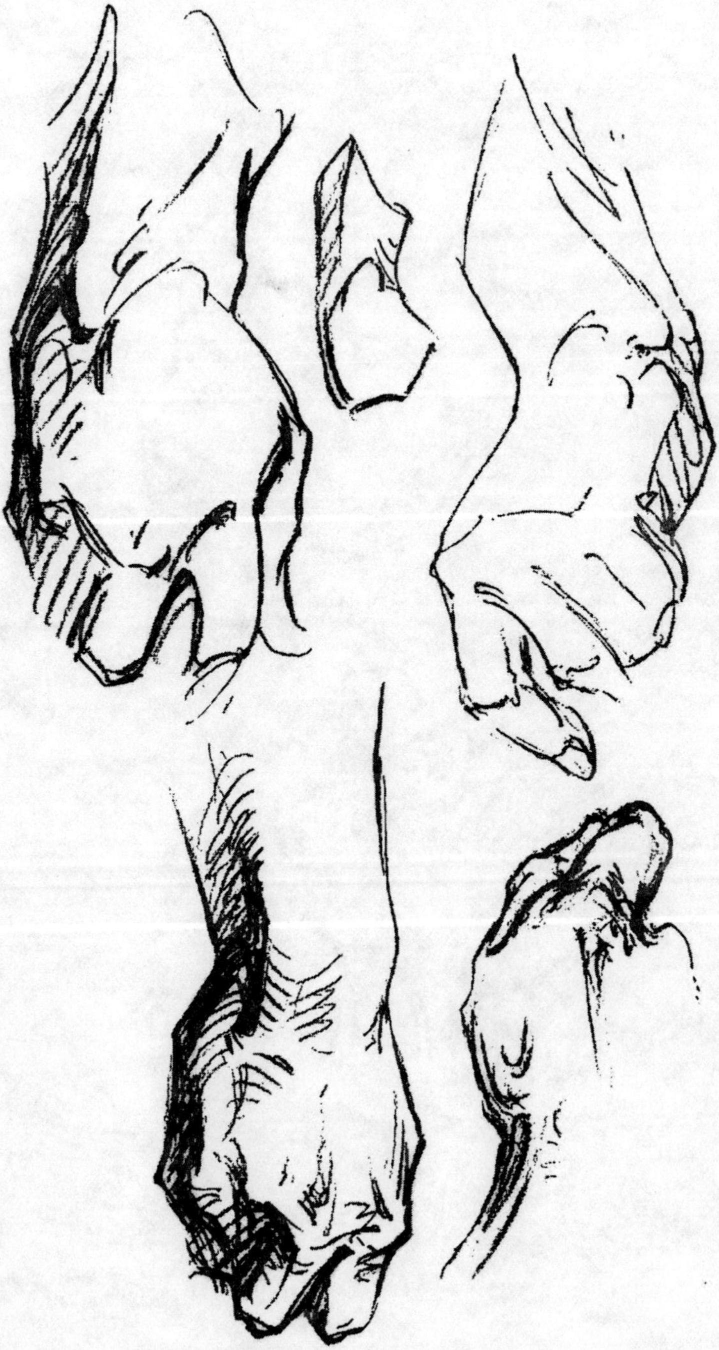

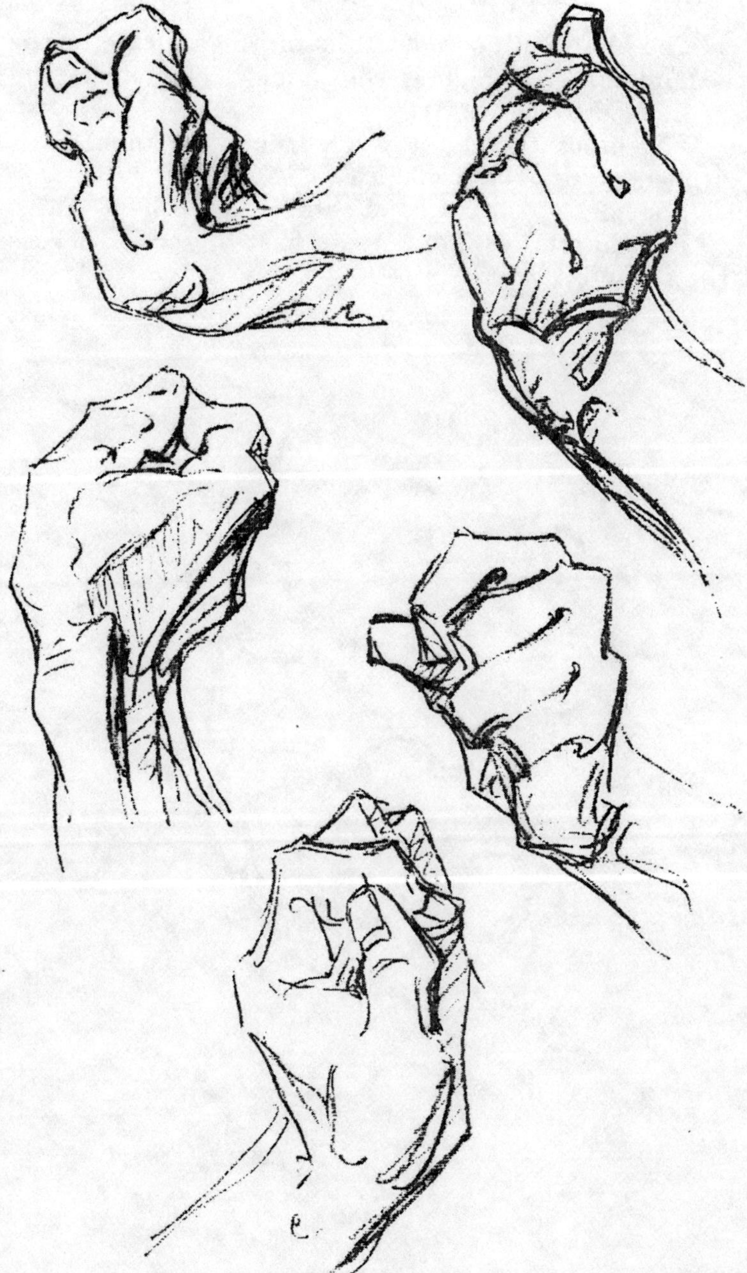

THE FIST

The blow with the fist falls on the knuckle of the second finger, which is the longest, strongest, and in line with the radius.

The more tightly it is clenched, the more it is arched across the knuckles.

The bones of the second row lie in the same plane.

The thumb lies against the first finger, or across the second.

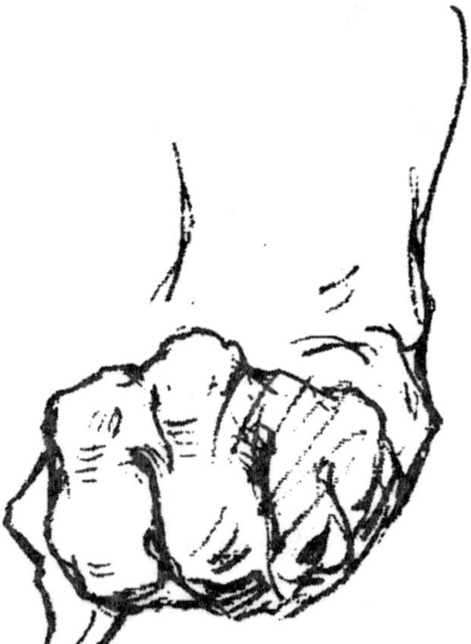

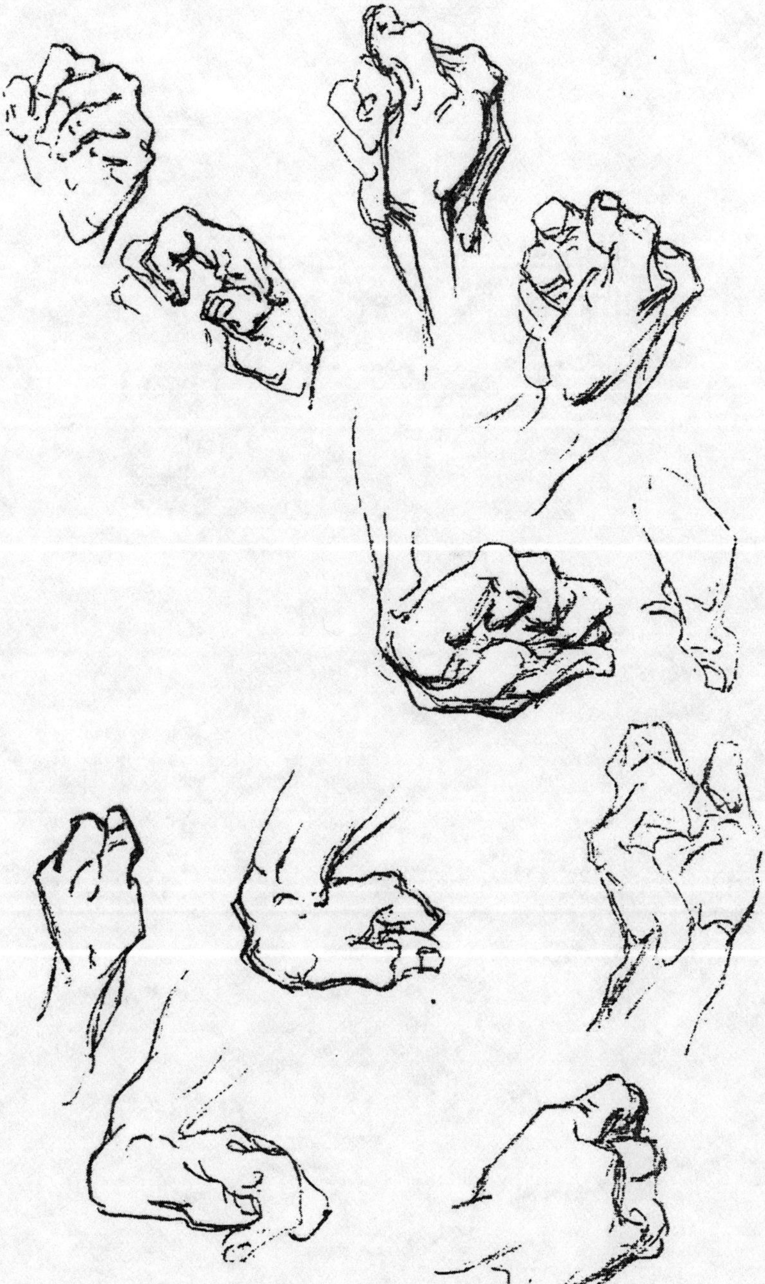

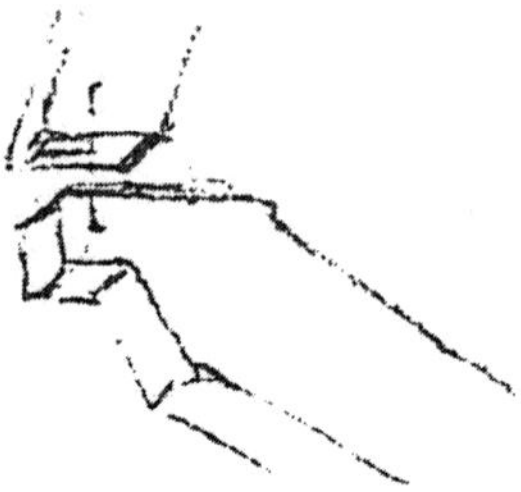

Mechanisms

From practically the same foundation grew on the hind leg a foot, and on the fore limb a hand. The foot, standardized to conditions of pressure, has massive bones with short toes and huge heel: has arches, columns, etc.

In the hand the determining factors were suspension or clasping, and movement. As the mechanics requires, the bones are long and slender, the fingers are long and flexible, with suspensory tendons running their length inside (i. e., next the object clasped); and the strong opposing thumb is warped around forward to complete the circle. The heel of the hand is negligible. The wrist is tapering, to allow freedom of movement.

The line of tension from the arm passes through the radius, to the wrist, thence in straight line to the middle finger, which is therefore the largest.

The thumb is warped around to the front corner of the wrist, covering at its base practically all of the side, and half of the front—the space opposite the bases of the first two fingers—and overlapping with its muscles the base of the third. Its attachment, in other words, is opposite the radius. It sweeps across the first three fingers.

The carpal bones are deeply arched backward across the wrist. This is to allow the flexor tendons to pass as near as possible to the point of least movement, in turning movements. Thus, in turning when the hand is clasped, there is little if any change of tension produced in these muscles by it.

From this point diverge the tendons to the fingers. This point is therefore the centre of symmetry for the fingers. From it they radiate; around it the knuckles, rows of joints and finger tips form concentric arches; and when bent, the fingers form transverse arches. The centre of these arches is slightly drawn toward the base of the thumb by its power, and the finger arches are somewhat altered by crowding.

The ends of this wrist arch are its pillars—the trapezium under the thumb, the pisiform under the little finger side. The arch is a little higher and broader under the thumb, on account of the greater power applied there.

At the four corners of the wrist are attached muscles. But as the wrist bends back in clasping, the bases of the first and second fingers at the back are brought into more direct line with the tension; wherefore the muscle of this corner is doubled, and the bones are larger.

As the hand in clasping bends back and the thumb forward, the bones of the wrist adapt themselves. The bones of the second layer bend with the hand; those of the first layer remain straight with the wrist, although those under the thumb of both layers curve around with it.

Between these two layers is therefore an angle; it is seen in profile as a hook, pointing upward at the back. In extension (as in clasping), the radius is straight against the end of the hook. With the hand straight it is against a corner of it, leaving a step-down over the hook to the back of the hand. In flexion, the end of the hook seems to add itself to the end of the radius, making a long convex curve to the hollow of the hook, beyond which is the mound of the metacarpals, and beyond that again the somewhat hollowed sweep to the knuckles.

The wrist attaches to the radius, and therefore

this hook, with the prominent metacarpals, is opposite the end of the radius—that is, a trifle to the thumb side. They become a ridge which turns slightly to follow the direction of the hand.

In its warping around, the thumb is not brought to face the hand, but faces across the palm; in position to bind down the ends of the fingers in clasping. Being on the radial side, yet drawn toward the mid line in traction, it makes the hand as a whole bend more easily to the little finger or ulnar side. Being in front, it causes the hand to bend more easily backward.

Turning movement as distinguished from rotary movement (flexion to each corner in rotation) is not present in the wrist, but is produced by the radius or turning bone of the forearm. Movement in the wrist is confined to flexion and extension (about one right angle) and side-bending (a little more than half a right angle, in the average hand); these two combined produce some rotary movement.

In movements of the wrist to extreme positions, the hand and fingers almost always participate, on account of association of tendons and muscular action; and in these positions it is practically always separation and hooking of the fingers that is produced.

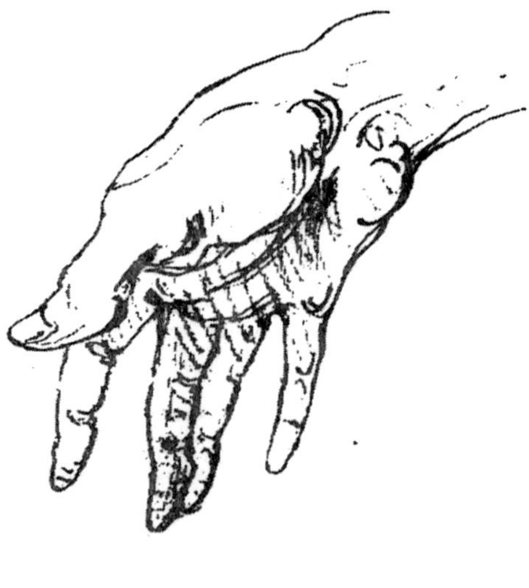

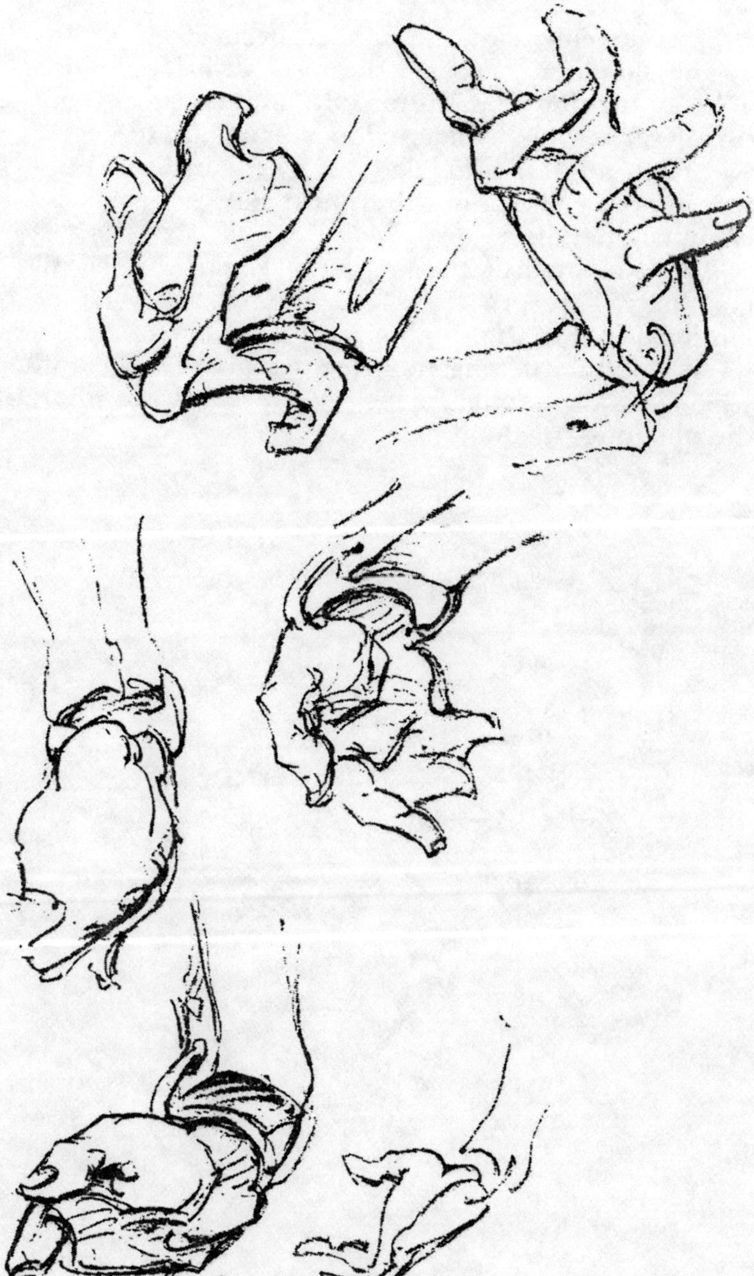

The movement of the hand reflects itself as far as the shoulder, through the biceps muscle, which aids in turning the radius. In all movement but turning, the wrist can act alone. Turning, to nearly two right angles, is carried out by the radius. Further movement of any kind must be performed by elbow or shoulder.

At the elbow it is the hinge movement that is important, wherefore the large size of the ulna or hinge bone, and the small size of the radius. At the wrist it is the turning movement that is important, wherefore the radius forms two-thirds of the joint, the ulna one-third.

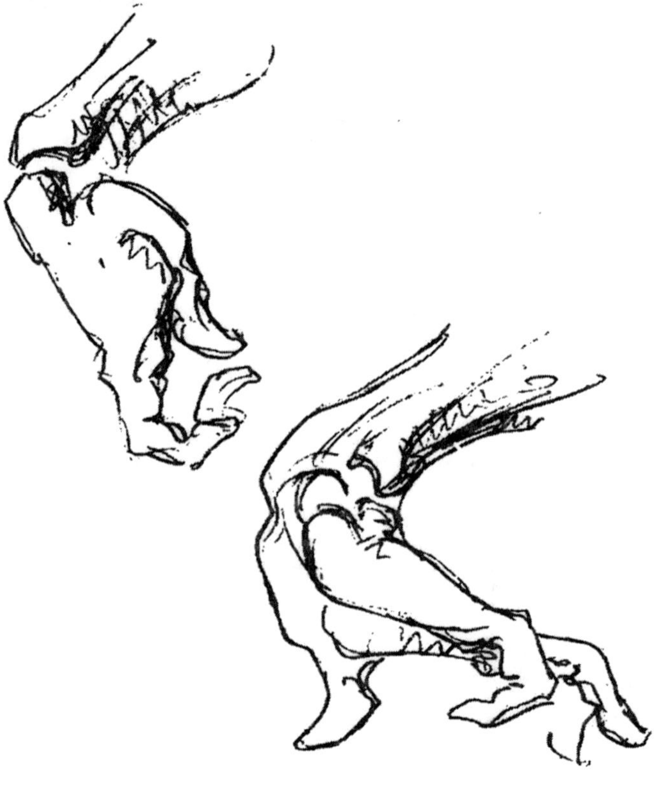

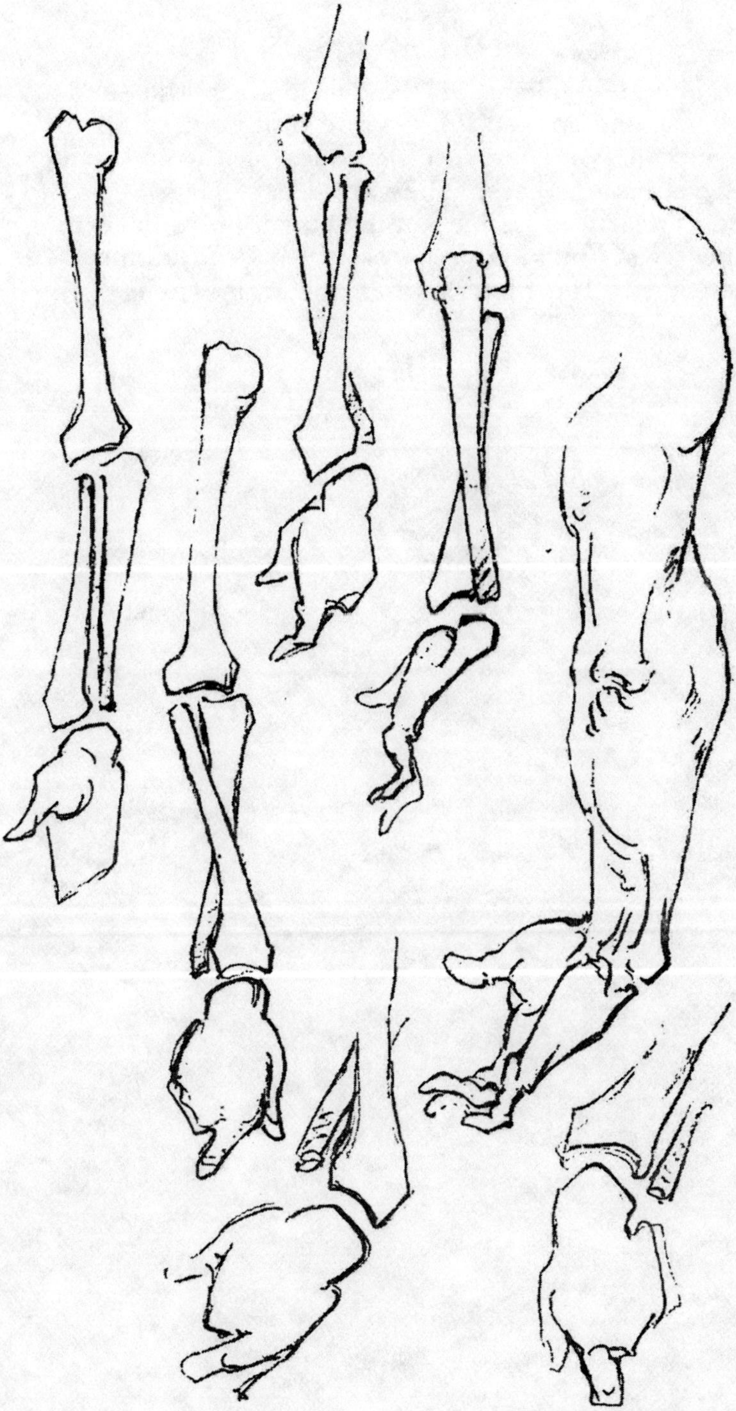

The two pillars of the wrist clasp the tendons almost like hooked fingers and thumb. The opening is closed by strong fascia into a ring through which these tendons pass. They are deeply placed so as to be as near as possible to the neutral point in turning the wrist, making unnecessary a readjustment of tension to the fingers when the wrist turns.

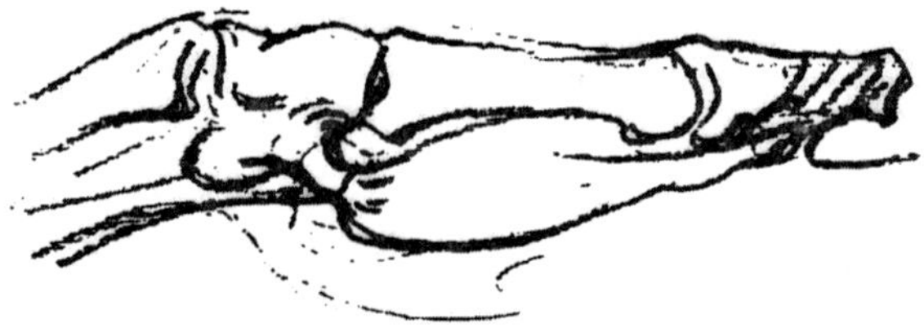

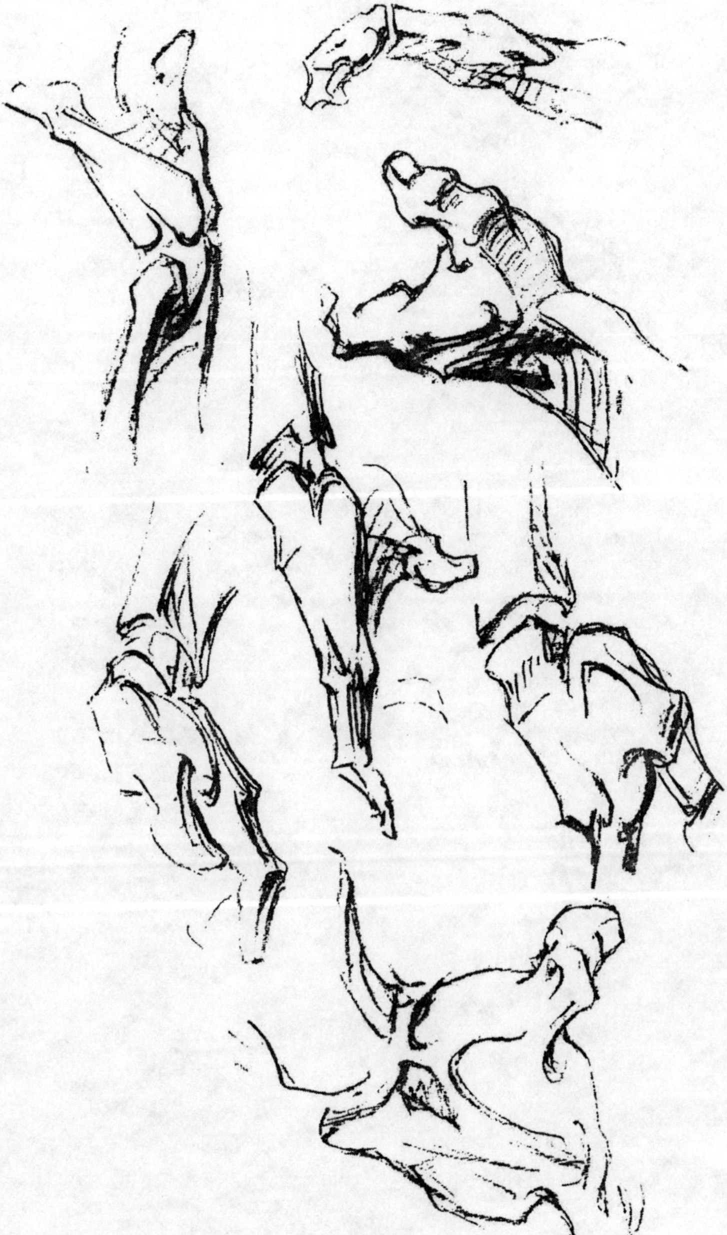

MECHANISMS

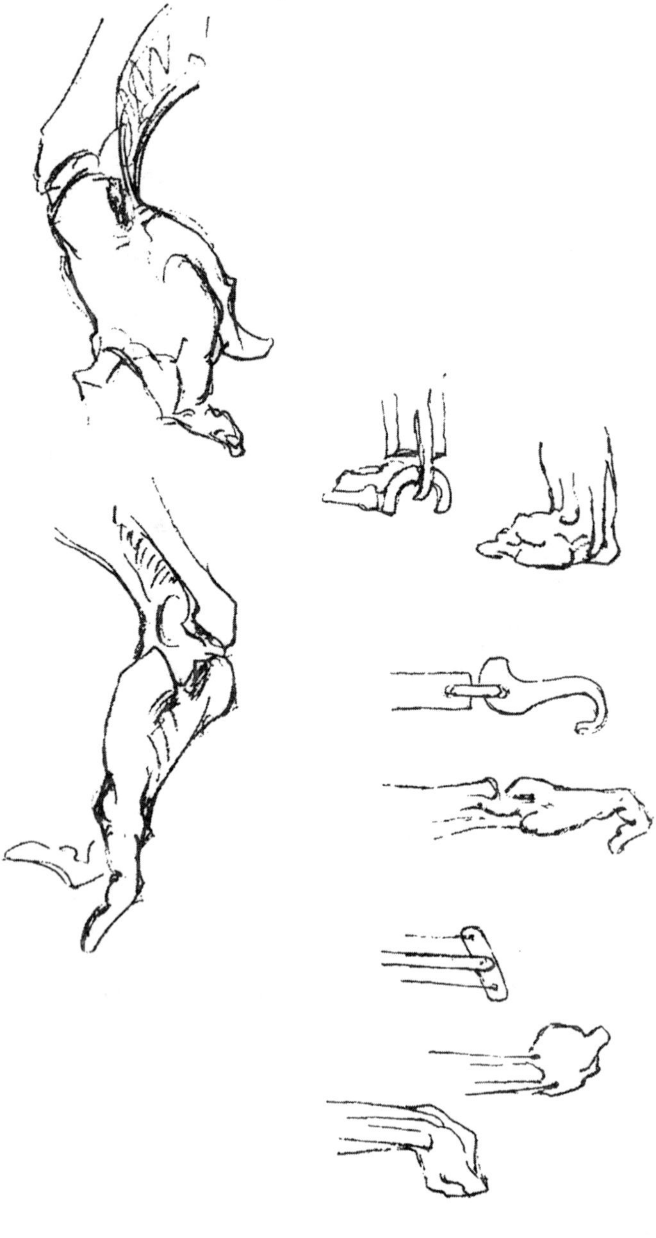

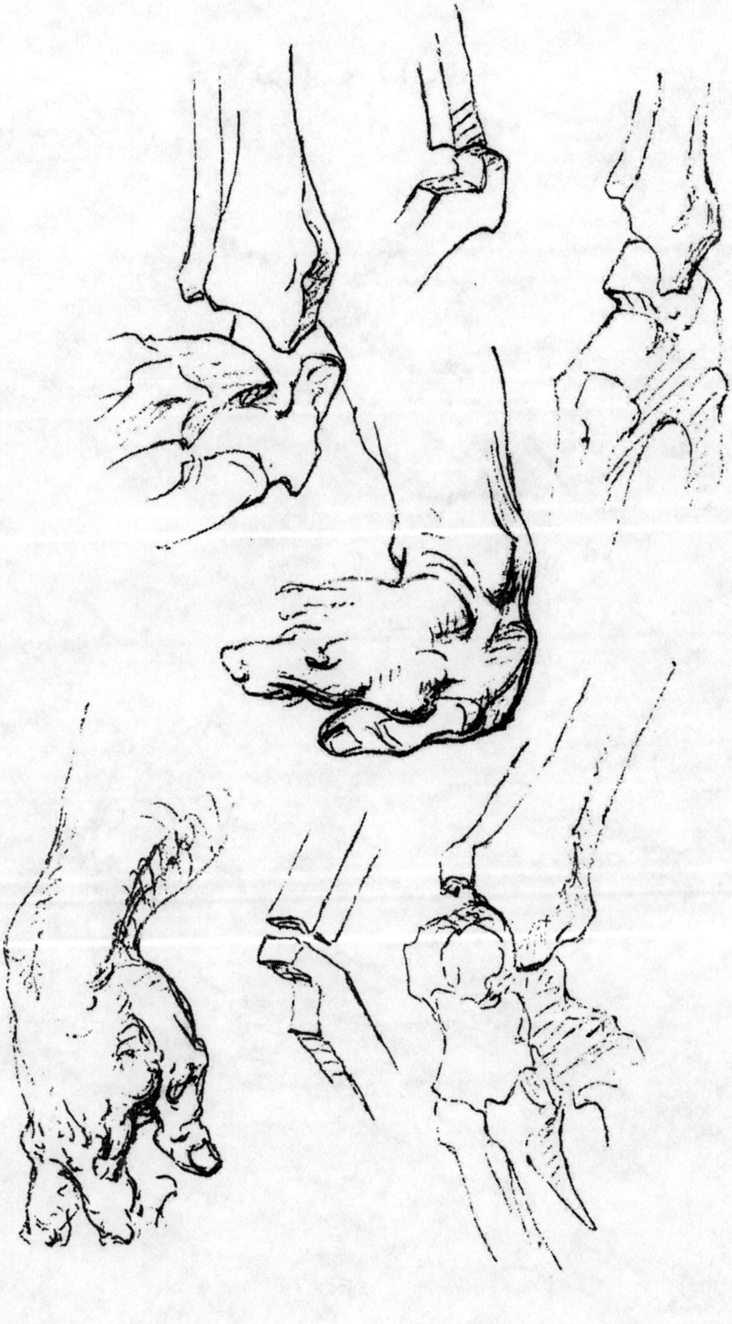

MECHANISMS

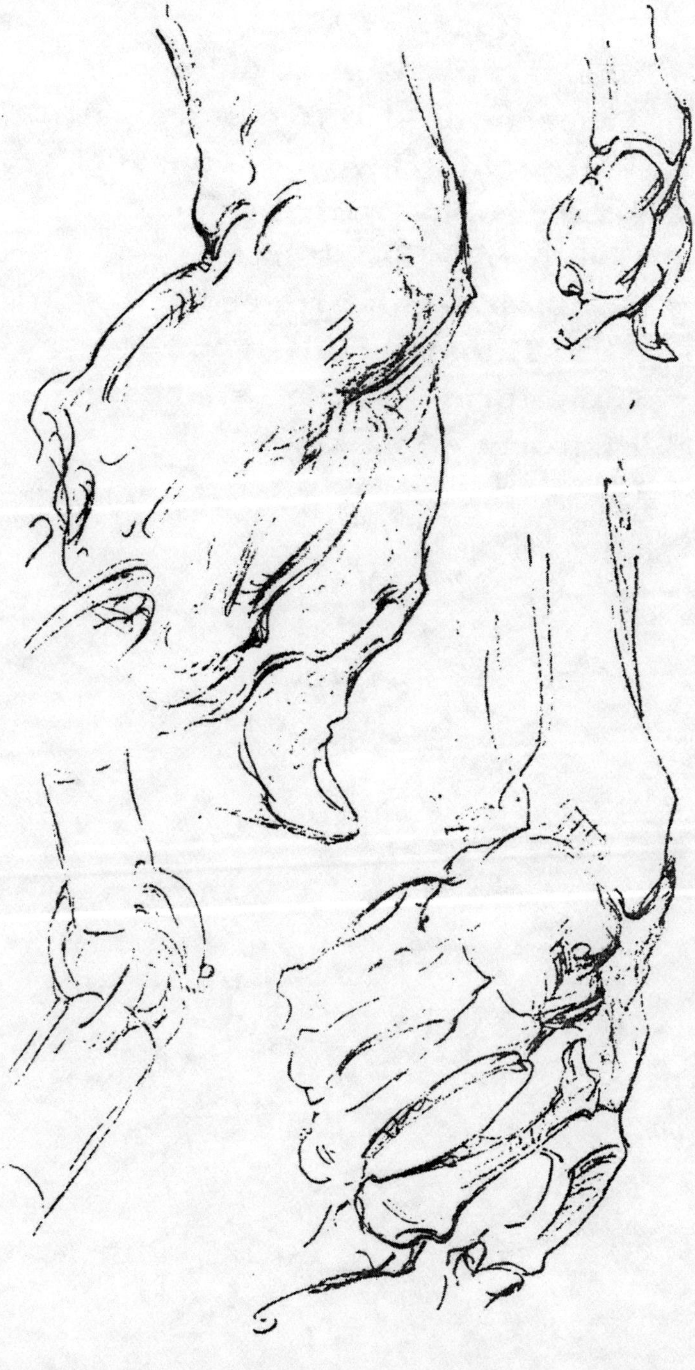

THE HAND

Bones of the Wrist, palm side:

1 Trapezium—No two sides parallel.

2 Trapezoid—Two sides parallel.

3 Os magnum—Great bone.

4 Unciform—Hook-like.

5 Scaphoid—Boat-shaped.

6 Semi-Lunar—Half-moon.

7 Cuneiform—Wedge-shaped.

8 Pisiform—Pea-shaped.

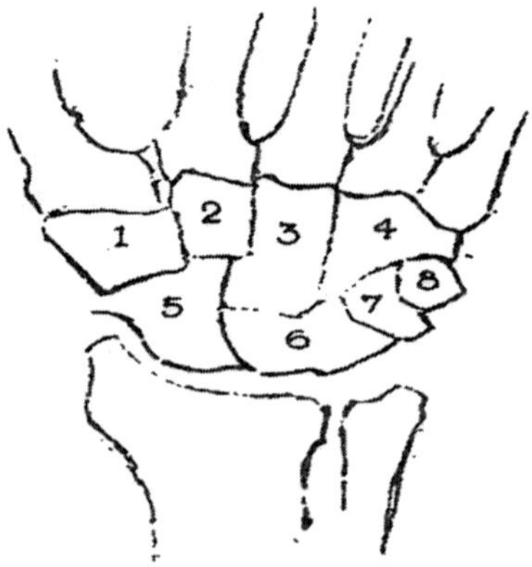

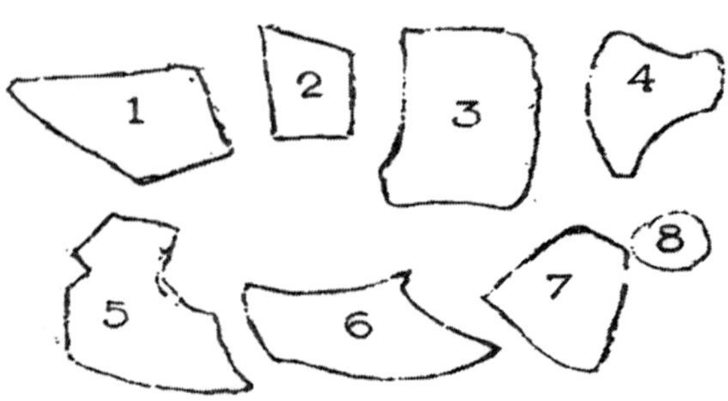

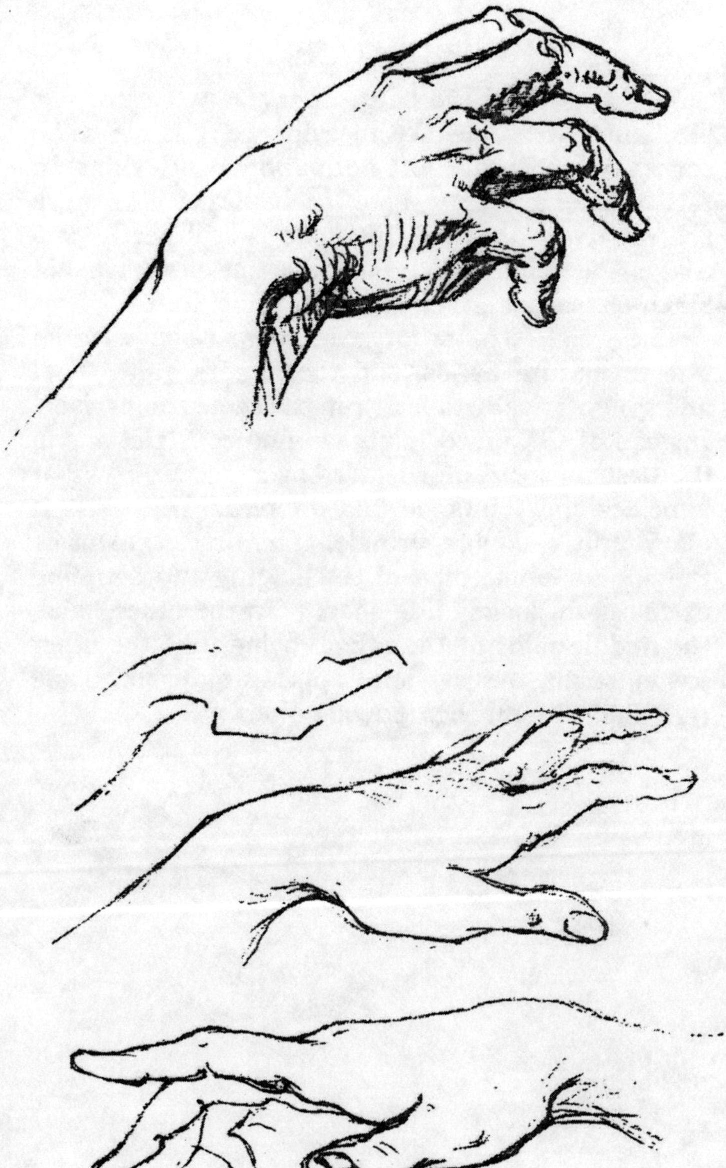

THE HAND

In the hand of the baby, neither anatomical nor mechanical features are in evidence, but are alike concealed under the soft flesh and smooth skin. In fact, neither anatomical nor mechanical features are sharply defined as yet; the bone is still partly cartilage, the joints still small, the muscles have not taken shape nor given shape to the skin.

The wrist is quite large in comparison with its size in mature hands, and the fingers quite short and symmetrically tapering in the same comparison. Instead of expanded joints we find constrictions in the flesh; instead of wrinkles over on the backs of knuckles and joints we find dimples. The wrist is marked by a double wrinkle. The first segment of the fingers, on account of the bulging and dimpling of the flesh, looks quite short. On the other hand, the middle joint of the thumb being, like the other joints, small, the last joint appears quite long, and the whole thumb has flowing lines.

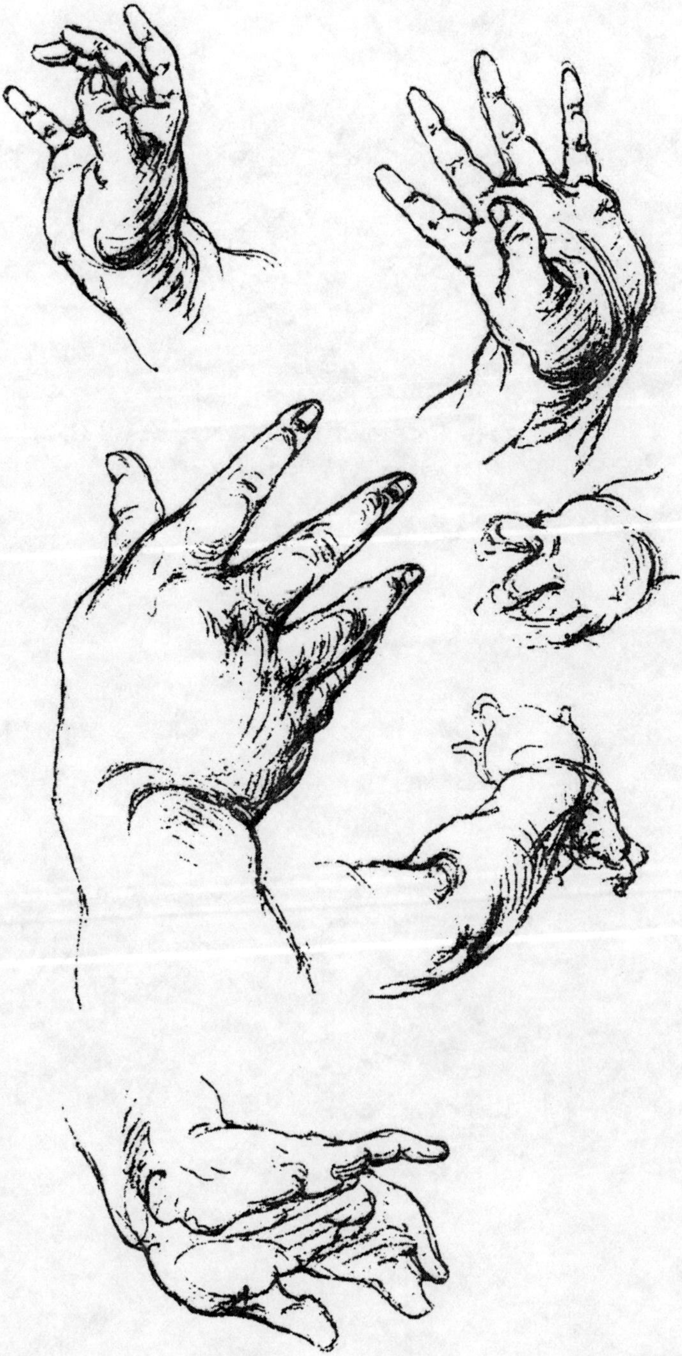

Origin, Insertion and Action of Muscles

Origin, Insertion and Action of Muscles

THE HAND—Back View

Abductor Minimi Digiti: Draws little finger away from hand; from pisiform bone to first phalanx of little finger.

Abductor Pollicis: Draws thumb from hand; from wrist bones and ligament, to first phalanx of thumb.

Dorsal Interossei: Between metacarpal bones, back side; from sides of metacarpals to bases of phalanges corresponding.

Extensor Brevis Pollicis: Short extensor of thumb; from back of radius to base of first phalanx of thumb.

Extensor Carpi Ulnaris: Extends wrist, ulnar side; from external condyle and ulna to base of fifth metacarpal.

Extensor Communis Digitorum: Common extensor to all the fingers; from external condyle of humerus to all of second and third phalanges.

Extensor Carpi Radialis Brevior; and

Extensor Carpi Radialis Longior: The long and short extensors of the wrist, radial side, representing the extensor that is doubled; from external condylar ridge of humerus to (5) base of second and third metacarpals, and (6) base of first metacarpal.

Extensor Longus Pollicis: Long extensor of thumb; from back of ulna to base of last phalanx of thumb.

Extensor Minimi Digiti: Extends little finger; from external condyle of humerus to second and third phalanges of little finger.

Extensor Ossis Metacarpi Pollicis: Extensor of metacarpal bone (first segment) of thumb; from back of radius and ulna, to base of metacarpal bone of thumb.

Origin, Insertion and Action of Muscles

THE HAND—PALMAR VIEW

ABDUCTOR MINIMI DIGITI (see page 169).

ABDUCTOR POLLICIS (see page 169).

ADDUCTOR TRANSVERSUS POLLICIS: Transverse (portion of) adductor muscle of thumb; from third metacarpal bone to first phalanx of thumb.

ANNULAR LIGAMENT of wrist; ligament that surrounds wrist like a bracelet; making with wrist arch a lesser ring for flexor tendons.

FLEXOR BREVIS MINIMI DIGITI: Flexes little finger; from wrist bone and ligament to first phalanx of little finger.

FLEXOR BREVIS POLLICIS: Short flexor of thumb; from wrist bones and annular ligament and bases of first three metacarpals to first phalanx of thumb.

FLEXOR CARPI RADIALIS: Flexor of wrist, radial side; from internal condyle of humerus to metacarpal bone of index finger.

FLEXOR CARPI ULNARIS: Flexor of wrist, ulnar side; from internal condyle, olecranon and ulna to annular ligament, pisiform and fifth metacarpal bones.

LUMBRICALES: Fore and outer parts of each tendon of the flexor profundus, with the corresponding interossei.

Opponens Pollicis: Draws thumb against fingers; from wrist bone and ligament to metacarpal bone of thumb.

Palmar Interossei: Draw fingers together; from palmar surfaces of second, fourth and fifth metacarpal bones to bases of corresponding phalanges.

Palmaris Longus: Long tensor of palmar fascia; from internal condyle to annular ligament and palmar fascia.

Supinator Longus: Flexes and turns in radius and hand; from external condyloid ridge to tip of radius.

INDEX